ZONZ

By: Josephine Jan Fritch

Josephine Jan Fritch is a mother of one, an artist, and a professional real estate agent. Since early childhood, she dreamed of writing a screenplay about advanced life from another planet that readers would fall in love with but put those dreams on hold to focus on her family and her career. After her divorce she finally plucked up the courage and made time to put pen to paper to create her first epic science fiction screenplay, which transformed into the novel *Zonz*.

ZONZ

Zonz is a work of fiction. Names, characters, places, and incidents either are the product of the author's imagination or are used fictitiously. Any resemblance to actual persons, living or deceased, events, or locales is entirely coincidental.

The author published, registered, and trademarked the *Zonz* book, story, cover, and art, and all designs and illustrations.

Copyright © 2011-2013 by Josephine Jan Fritch

Published in the United States by Josephine Jan Fritch, CA
The cataloging-in-publication data is on file at the Library of Congress.

ISBN-13: 978-0-692-01980-1
ISBN-10: 0692019804
Printed in the United States of America

Dedication

To all those who never stopped believing in me.
I am indebted to Kevin Alexander Shall.
Thanks for believing in me and for your constant support.

Advance Praise for *Zonz*

"It is perhaps the best of the epic fantasies. It takes you away on the most thrilling and magical adventure of your life! And it posits empowerment of human sexuality."
—James B. Marskell

"This original science fiction thriller is a magical experience! It will keep you in suspense, thrills, exhilaration; will touch you with its drama, mystery, humor, romance; and, above all, will take you away on the most thrilling and magical adventure of your life!"
—Teresa J. Montecelli

"In *Zonz*, author Josephine Jan Fritch blends heated sexuality, exploration, and mysterious epic adventure into the most unforgettable new novel featuring heroes from an advanced planet..."
—Nancy Costa

ZONZ

By: Josephine Jan Fritch

Prologue

*O*n a beautiful, sunny beach...

The skies are mostly clear with some low clouds. On these clouds, there are several faces talking in dramatic voices.

Face One says, "In a world such as this—full of greed—a society afflicted by cynicism, selfishness, and an erosion of civility, a society that has lost faith in its leaders and institutions and hungers for a greater sense of human connectedness, greed is destroying its beauty and the purpose for which it was created. Continuing in this direction, the Earth will be defeated. The Earth is heading in the wrong direction. Destruction is inevitable, unless some major changes take place."

Face Two adds, "We can no longer allow humans to pursue ends that merely further endanger the future safety of this planet called Earth. This kind of wisdom turned to greed and destruction of the life-sustaining capacities of the planet; this will seriously maim Planet Earth. If the future safety of this planet is to be ensured, a change must take place—and now."

Face Three nods. "Every species on this planet goes back to the beginning of life and, in a broader sense, to the beginning of the universe. This planet is like a living being, and the evolving world is something sacred."

Face Four says, "We must confront the now-mature adult whom we've been preparing for this extremely important project. She's familiar with our voices; she has heard them ever since she was a little girl. She's grown up under these very clouds, heard our many conversations."

✳ ✳ ✳

Beneath the clouds, on the warm, sandy beach, a little girl is playing with seashells while these faces are talking right above her. The girl notices the faces and hears their discussion but continues playing.

✳ ✳ ✳

Face One says, "Even the smallest of peasants can change the future. We have guided, prepared, and molded this child into a mature adult for this project, and now its time has come."

CHAPTER ONE

It was Christmas morning at J. J.'s house, and all the presents were wrapped and under the Christmas tree, ready for her family, who was coming to visit on this day. It was all ready—except for J. J.

She got out of the shower and put on a robe. Her hair wet, she was feeling very lonely as she looked at the Christmas tree. She thought out loud, "There will be magic for everyone else when they open the presents, but there's no magic for me anymore in life." She felt lifeless and sad.

She was looking out into the backyard, staring through the French doors in her bedroom. All looked gray and gloomy; the sky was overcast, and the fog was thick, but she could see an apple tree, gray and without leaves, about twenty feet away. She was feeling lonely and depressed.

All of a sudden, a shining star appeared right in the center of the apple tree. It was sizzling;

lights shot from the bottom to the top, like a huge, sparkling diamond radiating silver light upward in long rays (about five feet wide and not quite as high). It felt like the star was full of energy, like it was something happy. It gave her a positive feeling, but J.J. didn't want to blink for fear that it would disappear, and she kept on staring at it without closing her eyes once.

Then it just disappeared. J. J. tried to be logical about it, but nothing seemed to resemble or explain this shining, sparkling, star-like thing. It left her wondering what it could have been.

Strangely, she felt that somehow she had overcome her depression, and she started feeling somewhat energized, as if the sizzling star had had an unexplainable effect on her. At that moment, something in her had changed, and she was now in a more positive and happier mood. It seemed that something had pulled her out of the quicksand of depression in which she had been stuck. She now had a branch with which to pull herself out.

＊＊＊

In one of the best rooms of the Marriott hotel, a real estate agency hosted a celebration at which they awarded the most productive realtors with trophies. J. J.'s friend Marcia received an award for earning more than one million dollars in commissions for the year.

J. J. was happy for her friend. "Congratulations! I haven't seen you in about two years. You have changed dramatically, Marcia. Tell me all about it. What changed you?"

Marcia whispered, "I did the seminar."

"You did the seminar?" said J. J. "What seminar? I want to know all about it. Ha, ha."

Before Marcia could respond, others interrupted their conversation, and Marcia said, "See you later, J. J."

J. J. spotted another of her friends, Phoebe, and walked over to join her. "Marcia was never that good in real estate, so what happened to her?" J. J. asked. "All of a sudden, she's so successful. She told me she did a seminar. What is it? Where is this place?"

"I know where it is," said Phoebe.

＊ ＊ ＊

J. J.'s newfound energy had left her determined to improve herself, and she decided to follow up on her Marcia's advice. She arrived at the *place*, and she told the lady behind the desk, "I want to register for *the seminar*."

CHAPTER TWO

In the corridor, there was an extended table covered with name tags. About six assistants were handing out the name tags to the participants and guiding them to a large room. It was approximately six in the evening.

In the large room were over two hundred people. Some were just walking in, others were already sitting down, and several were talking in groups. There were people of all ages (from eighteen and up), men, women, and people of different nationalities and from different walks of life and backgrounds. Some were dressed formally and others very casually—some, who knows? Suddenly, the loud voice of one of the assistants welcomed everyone to the seminar. Finally, the seminar's leader arrived and began speaking to the whole class. He introduced himself as Michael.

The room was filled with a palpable excitement. Everyone was a little nervous and wondering what was to come. They all had taken seats and were listening quietly. It seemed as if everyone who took the seminar was in the room. At the entrance, the assistant closed the large double doors, and the seminar began.

Michael introduced Miss Shantee Smith, who would present a part of the "Sex, Intimacy, and Relationships" class. The audience welcomed her. She asked the class to call her Shantee.

Shantee, a very soft-spoken, gorgeous lady in her midthirties, looked like a model. She addressed the class by saying, "This is just an introduction to your favorite class. Tonight, we'll start with human sexuality. Before we even talk about sex, I want to emphasize the importance of safe sex; it is just common sense. Since we know HIV is transmitted by bodily fluids entering another body, the sensible way to prevent infection is to block that entrance. Latex condoms, or 'rubbers,' have been proven to be the most effective prevention against HIV infection. Lambskin and other natural membrane products are not as good as latex. I just want to stress the fact that when having sex, protection is very important.

"I notice that as soon as we mentioned sex, it became very awkward and uncomfortable for many. But we're all sexual beings. Life on Earth is sexual for most living beings. I believe we should all know how our bodies function, so we can all be happier. I believe that lack of knowledge is ignorance.

"For now, we'll start with the ladies. Let's create a sexy new you, make you into an irresistible sex goddess. Great sex begins in your head. It also springs from a positive, confident, and sexy self-image. As I said, it all begins in your head. Even a beautiful woman will not be more than fleetingly attractive to a man if she is afraid to talk to him, can't look him in the eye, or slouches along, embarrassed by or frightened of her own assets. Her actions and words are clear signals that she isn't worth knowing because she doesn't think she is. But if she is confident, even if she has faults, she is magnetically attractive to everyone. You can ask a man to recall one trait that made the sexiest woman he ever knew so alluring. Invariably, he'll say it was her self-confidence. 'She carried herself with such confidence,' he'll say. If you know you're hot, others will see it in every move you make, even if you're not conventionally beautiful. Sexual electricity will crackle all around you. Your self-confidence is very erotic. If you believe you are the answer to a man's erotic dream, he'll believe it, too. Look at your sexuality as a secret gift. No other woman expresses her passion just the way you do. Feel your skin, hear the sound of your moans, imagine the look of passion in your eyes, and smell the scent of your excitement. These are all uniquely yours. No other woman has your unique qualities. No one moves like you do.

No other woman magically turns into satin at the briefest touch of his hand. Your sexuality is unique because you are unique. It is one of the most powerful, enduring, and creative forces on Earth. This tremendous power is yours to command, to enjoy, and to give as a very special and sacred gift. When you value yourself and the gift of your sexuality in this way, it becomes even more radiant and exciting. Your tantalizing glow literally gives off sparks.

"One of the greatest turn-ons for a man is to see how very much he's exciting you: he wants to know that his lovemaking is driving you wild in bed. The only way to arrange it so he stimulates you, and therefore himself, to the max is for you to know beforehand where all your sexual switches are and how they are turned on. Know thyself. If you aren't already familiar with your own body, take the time to start getting acquainted right now. Stand naked in front of a mirror. Investigate every inch of your body. Don't be judgmental; your objective is self-knowledge, not self-criticism. Note the sensuous slope of your breasts. Notice the difference between the two. Delight in the curve of your waist and hips, the swell of your abdomen, the strength of your legs. Get another mirror so you get a good view of your languorous back and fetching fanny. Note everything as if you were going to do a detailed drawing of your naked body from memory. Imagine every part in action, and then imagine every part from a man's point of view. See what happens when you touch yourself.

"Touch your skin, tickle yourself with a feather, and scrape your nails lightly across the surface. Message, knead, and caress yourself all over. Find out what feels best for you, what is most relaxing and most exciting. Fondle your breasts. Message them in circles with the flat of your palm. Twirl them between your fingers. Pull on the nipples. Watch them become erect and hard when you rub them with something smooth or cold or with hot water. Observe the sway and jiggle of your breasts. Imagine how a man would react to the feel and look of them. What would you want him to do with them? Try yourself. Go over your entire body in this fashion, observing and feeling everything that happens and imagining how a man would see it, feel about it, and react to it.

"Inspect your genitalia. Scrutinize your clitoris and vaginal opening. Feel the smoothness, the bumps, and the valleys. Squeeze your finger with your vaginal muscles, and see how it feels. Move to the clitoris, and with your fingers, circle it gently. How does it feel to insert a finger into your vagina at the same time as you are massaging your clitoris? What can you dream up to make it feel even better? Besides being immensely pleasurable, masturbation keeps your sex muscles in shape and is the best way to find out what really turns you on. Once you know your own sexual preferences, you can show your man how to satisfy them. Nothing turns a guy on more than watching and feeling a lovely woman writhe with sexual pleasure under his fingers and tongue. So be creative and adventurous when you explore all the possibilities of your libido.

"If you carry yourself with confidence, knowing you're the most interesting and alluring vamp in town, men will be drawn to you like a magnet. And once you're between the sheets, if you are secure in the knowledge that you can drive him really wild in bed, you will. The most direct way to a man's libido is to focus your attention completely on him and only him. Forget about any disagreements you had earlier. Don't waste time and energy worrying whether your hair looks good mussed or if your hand would be better off on his knee rather than on his elbow. Focus your attention on him. Cherish your lover's unique sexuality, and he'll feel like an adored king. Feel his manly chest, his adorable derriere, his playful penis. Make him feel that no one else exists for you. No one could possibly be a better, more exciting lover than he is. Let him see that he has truly swept you away with desire. When you forget yourself and start concentrating instead on your man, you'll find yourself automatically doing wonderfully provocative things to him. They will come naturally to you because of your heightened sexual awareness. You'll do just the things that excite him—not because you have to or because you've painstakingly selected them from your mental bag of sex tricks, but most important, because you just *want* to. Be a sex goddess. Make him feel wanted, relaxed, sexy, soothed, ecstatic—as if you can't get enough of him. Fondle him. Caress him. Kiss him lavishly. Lick and nibble him all over. Tell him he's handsome, strong, hard, irresistible, sexy, a wonderful lover, and that he's driving you wild with desire. And mean it! Abandon yourself totally to the joyful task of giving him pleasure; you'll find yourself getting more out of it than he does!

"Give him a spectacular orgasm by way of your hand, mouth, or vagina. Keep your man's penile skin stretched tight the entire time you are having intercourse or stroking by hand or mouth by holding the skin down with your fingers at the base. This magic maneuver can send him skyward! Keep up your stroking as he reaches orgasm but lightly. After he's ejaculated, confine your efforts to his scrotum and G-spot. Lightly pull on the shaft of his penis (stay away from the head), and massage his scrotum and perineum. This massage should feel to him as though you're milking him.

"Observe his responses very carefully, so you can give him even more of what he really likes. Every man has his own personal hot spots and turn-ons. It's good to find out what his are and play on them. Learn to read his pleasure barometer, so you'll know what to do more of. He may pant when he becomes very excited or moan and groan or start thrusting convulsively. Do unto him what he does unto you. Make mental notes of the special places he touches you and the way he does it, and then later, do the same to him.

"Get to know your man's personal preferences, so you can play him like a fiddle. The music you make will give both of you extraordinary pleasure. He just won't be able to help coming back for more. He will feel like no one else knows how to make him feel quite as good as you do. And you will see your sexuality as a sacred gift. The sexier you feel, the better you will be at enticing him into your bed.

"Use mental foreplay. Your brain is the most erotic part of your body. Remember that it's what goes on in your head that sets the tone, makes you feel and act sexy, and conjures up all the deliciously erotic things you're going to do.

"You know how aroused you can become when thinking about how you stroked your man's chest or his taut derriere or how he sucked your nipples the last time you were together. Well, he gets just as turned on thinking about your lovely warm vagina or the way you licked his ear last night. If you want to be an expert lover, you should practice the fine art of mental foreplay. Give him something to think about that will make him hot and bothered, something that will make him crazy to get his hands on you, something that will make him deliciously hard. Sex up his imagination, and you'll reap the erotic rewards.

Tell him about the self-massage, internal flexing, and voyeuristic activities you've been doing to get ready for him. Give him every luscious detail. Invite him to watch if you want.

"Show him some dirty pictures. The surest turn-ons are letting him watch you touch yourself in your G-spots and moan and shiver in front of him, pictures of women making love to each other, explicit shots of a man and woman having sex, or anything of that nature. Use your imagination.

"Another very sexy instrument is the phone—use it to call him unexpectedly at work or when he is out of town. Tell him you're going to spend all night sucking his erogenous zone. Go into juicy details and then hang up quickly. The sexual suspense will keep him hot for hours.

"No man can resist a woman who makes him feel like the sexiest, most desirable creature on the planet—the woman who treats him like an endless treasure house of delights. With you, he will always feel like the acme of male sexual prowess, a magical potentate capable of creating unknown ecstasies, a sex god playing with a luscious sex goddess. This is powerful stuff!

"This subject will continue. For now, we will take a break." She smiled.

CHAPTER THREE

In the corridor, there was a large clock on the wall. Two hours had passed. Four of the assistants were walking around getting things ready for the break. The double doors opened, and the crowd emerged with excited and somewhat confused expressions on their faces. They headed to the courtyard where there were marble benches and large potted plants.

The participants were all talking among themselves, discussing current events, sex, and relationships. Some men gathered together, talking about how they would like to learn what made a woman happy and about relationships. The men were discussing how cheating only existed if you got caught. What constituted cheating? They talked about how a man must seduce a woman mentally before he could seduce her sexually.

Alex approached J. J. He introduced himself. "Hi, J. J. You're in my group. Let's find the other five members and discuss the assignment together. As you know, Michael assigned a coach for every six participants, and I think our coach's name is George."

"I made a list of the names of everyone in our group," J. J. said. She showed the list to Alex.

1. J. J.: a full-time accountant and part-time real estate agent
2. Alex: land developer in his late fifties
3. Barbara: a bookkeeper in her late forties
4. Danielle: freelance photographer in her late twenties
5. Ronny: computer sales rep in his late forties to mid-fifties
6. Charles: medical student in his late twenties
7. Coach George: in his late thirties, works in an import-export family business

The group searched for each other. Finally, they were all together as a group and began introducing themselves. When Danielle and J. J. met, they became instant friends.

The whole group opened up about their lives, sort of bonded together, and told each other the kind of businesses they were in. They exchanged phone numbers. They discussed the possibilities of this seminar, as well as the strong character of Michael, the seminar leader.

Coach George approached the group. "Welcome, group! We need to schedule the time that each one of you will call me to discuss the possibilities of this seminar and how you are dealing with your homework and going about whatever changes you want to make in your life".

And so the group took turns scheduling a call time with the coach.

This was just one group of seven among over two hundred walking, talking people with smiling and serious faces.

While some people were having coffee, others were talking to each other. In one corner of the courtyard, there was a group of men and women talking about the class "Sex, Intimacy, and Relationships." J. J. and Danielle joined that group.

These men and women were very interested in learning about each other, about males and females, and what made people tick. One lady wanted to know how sexy started in one's head exactly. She wondered how an unattractive lady she knew attracted really wonderful men. They always swarmed around her. There was nothing sexy about her. What made her so sexy or even attractive to men? The lucky few who got her into bed were even more enamored after the heady experience of making love with her.

"This is what Miss Shantee was talking about!" she said. "This is a great class. I'd like to know more of Miss Shantee's secrets!"

J. J. responded, "Feel sexy, and you will be sexy. Sexy is in your head. No kidding. Try it and see. That's what Shantee was saying. Even if you're not felling particularly sexy at the moment, just conjure up your own sexy self-image. Pretty soon, you'll feel sexy. Send out warm, sensuous vibes a man can't help but pick up, and he won't even realize you're a little too short or too broad or too fat or too skinny; he'll see you as his own personal sex goddess. And in your sexy mood, you'll just naturally do and say wonderfully tit-illating things. Just the way you glance at his derriere will make his temperature—and other things—rise. I hope Miss Shantee Smith is staying. I'm going to try what she said!"

Danielle said, "I didn't know what sexy was either until I met a man who treated me like his sex goddess. He acted as if I were the most desirable woman on the planet, as if one look from me could drive him wild with desire. In bed, he taught me a lot about both our bodies—how they move, what they feel, how beautiful they are. I grew to love my body for how it could make me feel instead of being embarrassed about its shortcomings. I learned to see the incredible beauty and sensuous strength in a man's body, too. I began looking at myself in a different way, and men looked at me differently, too. I think they could feel my sexy thoughts and wanted to be part of them. We parted a year later, but the erotic feelings he brought to my life remained alive. And, yes, in order to be sexy, all you have to do is *feel* sexy."

One man stated that the reason he took the class was to learn how to please a woman sexually and that he had no clue what women wanted.

Danielle, standing next to J. J., responded by saying, "You men are so stupid! You're about middle-aged now, right? I would think by now in this time in your life, you would know how. I guess some men live all their lives without ever knowing how to please a woman sexually."

The man, whose name was Peter, looked embarrassed but replied, "There's lots of books that talk about a lot of things to do and all these different roles to play and positions, but none about how to give a woman an orgasm! Or the exact buttons to push!"

Peter continued, "Incidentally, since you say you have experience, are you going to tell me?" Sarcastically, he added, "Or are you just teasing me? Actually, are you teasing all of us in this group?"

Everyone in the group gathered a little closer, listening with big expectations and big eyes.

They were all tuned in so intensely, like they had never concentrated this hard before.

Excitement mounted in every person, and they all gathered around to hear Danielle's response, not caring if they were going to need intensive therapy for the embarrassment afterward.

As Danielle started to talk, they formed a tighter circle and listened intently.

"OK," Danielle explained, "it is true that as soon as people talk about sex, everyone starts to feel awkward and uncomfortable, but we are all sexual. We are all sexual human beings. Life on Earth is sexual for all living things. I believe that we should all know how the body functions, so we can all be happy. As Shantee pointed out, being shy or lacking knowledge is ignorance! We're all adults here, and this is for consenting adults, right?"

Everyone agreed.

Danielle continued, "I guess that nowadays we're all moving so fast, like we have fast food and fast sex. We're becoming somewhat like robots, and we don't even know it. We don't pay much attention to how we or the other person feels. We don't have much time for romance or the feelings that come with romance.

"Think about when you were a teenager, and the girl was a virgin. She wanted to stay a virgin, but you both wanted to play, and your fingers gently tucked her hair behind her ear and then circled her ear. Very softly, rhythmically, you tugged her earlobe. You whispered things in her ear, something like how beautiful she is. It's so sexual. Remember how eager you were then to even touch the girl? You were tender, and that is how you should be. Call it 'play like she's a virgin.' Foreplay is very important to get both of you excited. Embrace her; cradle her head. Explore her mouth with your tongue. With your hands on either side of her face, stare intently into her eyes. Whisper fervently to her. Kiss her again, sweetly and passionately. Stare at her, blinking slightly.

"You can play all kinds of games or roles, but the most important thing is how you can give a woman an orgasm. I guess I can tell you two of the many ways a woman has an orgasm.

"For example, the woman's genitals are like her face. When you talk to a woman, her face is right in front you," Danielle continued. "Of course, you need to pay close attention to your partner. Be present to the moment. Watch her facial expression, and be very tender. Think of the nose as the clitoris. The mouth is, let's say, the VJ. Men's genitals, let's say, are the gun. Instead of engaging in regular sex first, wait and very gently move your gun (your erection) tantalizingly slowly. Massage the entire genital area, and place your hand on the top opening of the VJ right above the clitoris, press down firmly, push upward, and keep one hand there. With your gun, move up to the clitoris.

"Stimulate the 'nose' up and down. Press firmly, gently, languorously, slowly, and then faster. Thrust up and down, and once in a while, go into the 'mouth'—not all the way in, just slightly in and out, pushing against her—and back to the nose. Press firmly, insistently. Keep on playing. You can do a wide, circular motion, pressing sometimes gently and sometimes more aggressively. Up and down, thrust—it is immensely pleasurable. She will writhe with sexual pleasure. You can go upward or downward. Continue in this manner, and with the palms of your hands, gently caress her breasts; kiss and nip each one gently. Think of a hot dog and bun, and keep sliding, going back and forth and in the mouth. Gently kiss her lip. Breathe in her ear. Continue until she's lost in erotic torment, and then go faster and more aggressively until she climaxes.

"To find the second G-spot, look at the face as an example. Inside of the mouth, at the top of the mouth, right after the teeth, is a ridge. This is the second G-spot. Use the face as an example. If the VJ was the mouth, that's where the second G-spot would be.

"After she gets an orgasm, you should still be tender and cuddly. Then slowly ease into her and start to move fast, hard, and large. Thrusting into her with your gun, pound the second G-spot over and over as she explodes around you. Thrust hard until you both climax."

Peter said, "I will love you forever, Danielle." He kissed her hand.

CHAPTER FOUR

It had been time to go back to class twenty-five minutes earlier, but no one in this group even noticed. They were all so engrossed in the subject, a cannon could have gone off and they wouldn't have noticed it. All the guys were looking at Danielle with different eyes. They all had sexy smiles on their faces. They looked just like little boys eating candy when their mother had said no. When they noticed the time, they all returned to class.

When everyone was sitting in class, Michael started to speak. "Everybody get into a group. Let's all share what we want to get out of this seminar."

Danielle said, "J. J., can I call you tomorrow to talk about this?"

"Yes, sure," J. J. said. "Danielle, you do know that this seminar is for two months—once a week on Thursday night and six full Saturdays—right?"

"Yes, I know. Isn't it exiting?" Danielle whispered in J. J.'s ear, "I like the coach, don't you?"

J. J. whispered back, "I like Alex."
They both giggled.

They all exchanged phone numbers and discussed their hopes for the seminar.

Michael said, "Make sure that you all take the paper with the assignment for next week. It will be handed to you at the door as you leave. See you all next week."

Finally, the class had ended. They all said their good-byes and "See you next week!" as they walked to the parking lot.

Alex jokingly asked J. J., "This first class was powerful. Are you motivated yet?"
J. J. said, "I agree it was powerful. I'm so motivated that I could go on the freeway without a car and get a speeding ticket. Ha, ha!"
They both laughed.

Alex and J. J. said good night until the next week.

J. J. arrived home. Phoebe, the woman who rented a room from J. J. in her modern two-story home, was there along with their neighbor Samantha. The house was well decorated with lots of beautiful oil paintings hanging on the walls, painted by J. J. herself.

Phoebe and Sam were waiting in the living room. They shut off the TV when J. J. arrived.

Phoebe said, "J. J., I've been waiting for you. How was the first class? Did you like it? Did you meet any good-looking guys?"

Sam interjected, "Wait! Don't anyone say anything. Let me get some coffee first. J. J., do you want some coffee too?"

J. J. said, "Yes, I'll have some coffee. OK, there were over two hundred men and women in this class. The majority are men—good-looking men—and many are professional, well-educated people, or at least they look that way. And, oh yes, we have homework."

J. J. took off her coat. Sam came back with coffee for herself and J. J.

"You should see Michael, the seminar leader!" J. J. said. "Ooh but he's too young for me...Oh well. There are six people in my group. Alex is one of the participants, and he's so cute. There is this lady teacher whose name is Shantee. She talked about creating a sexy new you and making yourself into an irresistible sex goddess. You both should be taking this class with me! There was so much sexual tension among the group. I'm so tired. I'll tell you all about it tomorrow. I need to get some sleep. Good night, ladies!"

Phoebe said, "I'm going to bed too, J. J., but tomorrow, we are going to talk about your seminar!"

Sam added, "Good night. See you tomorrow."

✳ ✳ ✳

J. J. was sound asleep dreaming.

In her dream, she entered a glass-like castle where on one side, ancient Egyptians were dancing or participating in some kind of celebration. On the other side, there was a large, round crystal box. In the middle was a huge, lit-up crystal dome about ten feet in diameter. The room was like a huge, round crystal box with a glass door that opened when a huge bronzed man with very big muscles and a great physique touched the side of it with his hand. The glass door opened. J. J. thought it seemed like the fountain of youth, like something that would cure people when they passed through the door.

J. J. was so amused by this huge crystal box she kept on touching the outside of it and trying to push it. For some reason, she was trying to take it with her. It didn't make any sense.

She didn't know how she could, but she wanted—more like *needed*—to take it with her. Suddenly, J. J. noticed something was following her. As she was walking around, she saw a skinny stick, about three to four feet long and about a half to one inch around; it was about a foot above the ground, floating in the air, upright. It looked just like a crack in the air, so she didn't understand what it was. All of a sudden, an urge came over her to grab it and put it in her pocket, so she did.

Three huge men appeared and began chasing her. She ran out of the dome. She jumped in her rocket ship and sped through the stars and through the universe. While she was passing through some rock matter and small comets, three rocket ships began chasing after her. She was so scared she couldn't breathe. J. J. swerved and dodged the chasers, traveling as fast as the rocket ship would go. As she was speeding through the stars, despite her overwhelming fear, she couldn't help notice how colorful and breathtakingly beautiful all the shining stars around her were. She was fascinated by the play of colors in the universe.

After a long chase, those rocket ships were getting closer and closer to her. J. J. started to hyperventilate; she was terrified that she was about to be killed. A huge explosion occurred right behind her. It was as if someone had blown her up. It was like a bomb had exploded right behind her. She felt as if she were part of the huge explosion!

✳ ✳ ✳

Suddenly, J. J. woke up screaming in terror to discover it was only a dream—a nightmare!

J. J. was hyperventilating, barely able to catch her breath. She was soaked in sweat, the fear of death still with her. She got out of bed and dragged herself into the shower, turned the water on, and just sat on the shower floor with the water running over her, getting soaked and regaining her composure.

Phoebe rushed into J. J.'s room.

"J. J., are you OK? I heard you scream! I got you a glass of water!"

J. J. took the glass of water and drank it, still trying to catch her breath.

"Oh, I'm sorry I woke you up, Phoebe."

"Oh, honey, it's OK. I don't mind. You need to talk about these nightmares...to me or someone else. You can't go on like this! I'm afraid you're not going to be able to catch your breath one of these nights!"

Phoebe shut off the water, wrapped a towel around J. J.'s shoulders, and helped her to bed.

"How can I talk to anyone about this?" J. J. asked. "I don't understand these dreams myself. How can I explain them to someone else? These nightmares don't make sense to me. I'm afraid to tell anybody about them. People might think I'm crazy." J. J. took a few deep breaths. Slowly, she fell back to sleep.

The next morning, Sam came over for coffee. J. J., Phoebe, and Sam were drinking coffee, and there was a knock on the door. It was Sam's sister Rosy. Rosy was in her late forties.

Rosy said, "I dropped off your groceries. Here's your change. Every time I go to the store, everybody I know needs something."

Sam said, "Thanks, Sis. How are the boys?"

"Well, Denny is dating this slut. I hope they break up soon. I can't stand her. I just reminded Denny to make sure he uses condoms." She sat down on a chair.

"Well, Sis, Denny is twenty-one years old now, and besides, that's kind of a sensitive subject to discuss in front of his three brothers."

"Oh no, I've always been open with my boys, from when they were very young, even when my husband was alive. You know—this was a long time ago—I was shopping at Costco, and in this large shopping cart, there were sales items, including this large box of condoms on sale for ninety-nine cents, so I bought it. Ninety-nine cents, can you believe it? When I got home, I told my boys that they should use protection for health reasons and gave them the box of condoms. I encouraged them to always use protection, especially at these prices! Ninety-nine cents! You can't go wrong. John, my oldest son, told me that they do use protection. He said, 'Look at the box, Mom; it's size *large*. These are too big! That's why these condoms are ninety-nine cents. Nobody wears size large. We can wrap one of these condoms all the way around Denny.' Denny wasn't there at the time. I didn't know that. I thought all men were size large! Who knew? Oh, you should have seen my face turn red."

They all laughed—except for Rosy.

"My point is that I've always been open with my boys, especially when talking about sex. Well, I got to go. See you all tomorrow."

Sam, J. J., and Phoebe all said good-bye to Rosy.

"Well," Sam said, "I've got to put the groceries away. See you all later."

She left the house.

✳ ✳ ✳

In the kitchen, J. J. was having coffee with Phoebe when the phone rang. It was Danielle.

"Hi, Danielle," J. J. said. "We are? OK, I'll put it on my calendar." She turned to Phoebe. "We are going to meet on Sunday afternoon at the Seaside Café, the whole group."

"Can I come too?" Phoebe asked.

"Can my friend Phoebe come too?" she asked Danielle. "Oh, OK! I'll tell her...Thanks! See you Sunday." She hung up the phone.

Phoebe asked, "Who is Danielle?"

"She's in my group. She told me about the meeting on Sunday, and yes, you can come too. I'm exhausted from not being able to sleep. I need some sleep today."

Phoebe asked, "Promise me you'll go see someone about your dreams, a dream analyst or a psychiatrist. You have to...Please, J. J., I'm afraid these nightmares are going to kill you. Please promise? My brother used to have nightmares, and he went to a psychiatrist."

J. J. said, "Well...Phoebe, I promise that I will talk to someone about it—but not a shrink!"

"OK, just talk to someone and talk to me too. We're friends; I will keep it a secret."

Sam came in, got a cup of coffee, and joined J. J. and Phoebe.

Sam said, "I'm going on a date tonight, and I don't have a thing to wear. J. J., can I borrow your black dress with the wrap? It looks great on me."

"Who's your date, Sam?" Phoebe asked.

"He's a psychologist! He's tall and cute. My cousins introduced us. James is his name. He asked me out right then and there, and I said yes."

Phoebe said, "Psychologists and psychiatrists, they are all crazy people. That's why they become psychiatrists! Because they know how it is to be crazy. No one knows better than they do because they went through it. They were schizos, you know, Sam? Ask your friend what level of craziness he was at before he went to get his degree."

"Sam, don't listen to her," J. J. said. "She's just joking...She's teasing you."

With a confused look on her face, Sam asked, "You really think he was crazy before he got his degree?"

"Sam, Phoebe is just trying to scare you. Don't listen to her."

Phoebe said, "A long time ago, I used to work for a company that handled mental health insurance, and they had all of these crazy people applying for degrees in psychiatry; most of them got it because they had actual experience with mental illness. The entire psychiatric department had a history of different levels of craziness...I'm telling you."

"And you want me to tell my dreams to the crazy people, huh?" said J. J.

"Uh-oh, I'm having second thoughts here," Sam said.

"Yes, Sam," J. J. said. "You can borrow my dress. I've got to go to work; first is the accounting job and then real estate. I have to show a few houses today. See you all later." J. J. went out the door.

CHAPTER FIVE

It was Saturday night. J. J. was sound asleep. She found herself again in the middle of the nightmare. J. J. was back on the Crystal Planet trying to steal the huge crystal box again. Suddenly, she started to wonder, *How did I get here?* Then again, the ancient Egyptian man came forward. This time, she was talking to him instead of running away from him.

"Why are you chasing me?" J. J. asked. "I know it looks like I was going to steal the huge crystal box, but there is no possible way that I could do that! The box is too big for me even to move, and then how would I fit it in my small rocket ship? It doesn't make any sense."

Now the other two Egyptian men came over, and without saying a single word, the three of them surrounded J. J. and guided her to a glass enclosure. It seemed like an elevator, and suddenly, she was someplace else.

J. J. was so scared that her hands and knees were shaking, and a voice inside of her was saying, "This is my dream, and I should be able to do whatever I like. What could happen? I'll probably wake up."

Then, a bald-headed man in a white robe, like those worn by government officials in historical eras, slowly appeared in front of her. He seemed very faded, and everything was white. There was so much light that J. J. could hardly make out all of his features. She suddenly started to hum. "Humn-humn-hm." She couldn't get any real words out.

The man made a gesture with his hand for J. J. to sit down on this cloud-like pillow.

While J. J. was sitting down, she was trying to wake herself up by slapping her face and telling herself to wake up.

No luck, her eyes felt like they were popping out of her head.

The man said, "Hello, J. J. I am Zavor."

J. J. practically jumped out of her skin. "You know my name? Who are you? Where am I?" J. J. was terrified and very tense.

Zavor said in a very loud but still somehow gentle and echoing voice, "You are from Zonz... Zone One. You call it Earth. I call it Zonz."

J. J. said, "The only 'Zone' I know is a diet! You know, there's a book called the *Zone*; it's a diet book."

"I am not talking about any diet!" Zavor said. "There are many planets. Yours is Zone One. Another planet is Zone Two, another is called Zone Three, and so on. After all the Zonz, there is this planet, the one we're on now. Do you understand?"

"No...Yes...Maybe...I mean..." J. J. stuttered and cleared her throat. "You call planets 'zones' instead of Earth, Venus, Mars, Pluto, right?"

"No! Human souls travel from Zone One to Zone Two, and after they have traveled through all the zones—Zonz—they come here. Do you understand now?"

"Is this heaven or someplace like that?"

Zavor said, "I don't know about your 'heaven or someplace like that.' This planet called Bingodarian, or Crystal Planet."

J. J. took a big breath. "I hope I can remember all this when I wake up!" she said, her left hand touching her forehead.

Zavor said, "Yes, you will remember all this... J. J., you are not dreaming; you are here. Your soul is here right now."

"I'm so confused..." J. J. said with both hands on her face. "Why did my soul come here right now? Why not stay on Earth...or Zonz, as you call it?"

Zavor said, "Because I sent for you...and you arc here body and soul right now."

J. J. said, "Is my soul dying? Is that why it's here now? Am I dying? Or am I dead?"

"*No*...your soul is not dying. The body dies; the soul transforms. It's not your time to die just yet. You're still needed on Zonz. You've had many close calls. Do you remember them?"

"No...I...I don't know?" J. J. was very confused.

Zavor said, "Look at the screen, and watch what happened when you were five years old."

A screen appeared out of nowhere, and there was a movie of J. J. when she was five years old. It was something that had happened when she was five years old. She was visiting her grandparents' farm. There was a storage room, and this girl who was about seventeen and her mother were there. J. J. wanted to swing on a single swing, which was hanging on a hook from the ceiling next to a corner of the room. The girl was angry that J. J. was using the swing, which she considered to be hers. She started to swing her very fast, bouncing J. J. off the walls, hitting her head and face on the wall very hard. J. J. was yelling, and her parents came to rescue her. She could remember well now how she could see herself from a distance. Her father was carrying her in his arms. He took her outside into the open. J. J.'s head and face were covered with blood. She looked dead, and many of her relatives were there; some were crying.

J. J. watched it all from a distance. Now she could see it like it was a movie that Zavor was showing her. She guessed that was what they called an out-of-body experience, and Zavor was trying to show her something.

Another memory started to play on the screen. J. J. was six years old. Her cousin, who at the time was twenty-six years old, took her with him to his vineyard about three or four miles away. They walked to the vineyard with her mother's permission.

When they were on their way there, his girl-friend, who happened to cross their path, stopped and they talked. Then she broke up with him in a very arrogant way. She mocked him, saying that his girlfriends were getting younger and younger, looking at J. J. He looked very pale and upset. He took two flowers from a nearby tree. They were very similar, and he gave her one and J. J. one. She commented on how similar the two flowers were, and how well he took the breakup, and then they left.

She went in a different direction. They went to this empty field near the path before the grapevines. He started to dig a huge hole in the ground. It was the size of a coffin and very deep. He stood up in it, and it was up to his head. He had taken his shirt off and was all sweaty and dirty. He wanted J. J. to get into the hole, but she refused, so he climbed out and pushed her into the hole. Then he hit her all over, especially on her head, until she was dizzy. He put a long stick in upright and tied J. J. to it, so she was stand-ing up in the grave. Then he filled the entire hole with the loose dirt up to her neck. He pounded the dirt all around her with his shovel. She was now buried in the grave with just her head and her right hand showing. In her hand was the flower that he had given her. He wanted J. J. to hold up the flower. He cursed her out and called her all kinds of horrible names. Whatever he wanted to say and do to the girlfriend, he did to her. He substituted J. J. for his girlfriend. At the age of six, J. J. didn't understand that at all. She thought it was about her. This haunted her most of her life until she was trying to do her home-work for a self-improvement class, and then it all surfaced. He told J. J. not to scream, or he would put tape on her mouth. He told her this was one secret that she would never tell or remember.

J. J. agreed with all he said so that he would stop yelling and hurting her. He put some flat wood on top of the outside of the grave, covered it, and leveled it with the outside ground to cover up the hole and then more dirt came in and bur-ied her alive.

J. J.'s cousin had taken her with him in the early morning; that was when he buried her alive.

That evening, a small group of farmer's help-ers who had had a job that day were on their way home when they heard a small child crying, so they spread out and searched.

One of the ladies found the ground with freshly dug soil and told them to dig there. After digging for a while, they found J. J.'s hand hold-ing a flower, and then they found her head and dug her out. Just before they took her home, her cousin (the sick individual) appeared. He was upset that someone had found her.

The man was holding J. J. passed her to another man so he could chase her cousin. Then the man who was holding her wiped the dirt off her face and told her to look at who had saved her life. She did, and although it was getting dark, she could still see. It was a family—some men, women, children, and teenagers. The women all had headscarves on. Then she passed out. One of the men chased her cousin, and the rest took her home.

J. J. was in a coma for two months. When she came to, she had to relearn how to speak because her voice box was so damaged.

Another happening in J. J.'s life flashed on the screen. When she was six and a half years old, she was in school, and there was a girl, one year older than J. J., named Teresa. Everyone thought the two girls looked alike, including Teresa's grandmother, who was a schoolteacher at that time. They were all in uniforms, and they played together. The teacher thought J. J. was Teresa and that Teresa was J. J. They could fool her very easily.

J. J. was great at math. Teresa was great at reading, and she was not. When she didn't have the answer to a math question, Teresa said she was J. J., and J. J. said she was Teresa. When J. J. couldn't read certain big words, Teresa would do it, and the teacher believed it was J. J. Teresa and

J. J. were so excited that they could fool people with their identity. They had so much fun.

One day at school, during a break, a mean girl told J. J. that Teresa was dead. Of course, J. J. didn't believe her, so she went to see for herself. She went to Teresa's house. When she walked into the room, Teresa was lying on a bed, dressed in an eggshell or off-white lace dress. J. J. thought she was asleep. She thought all she had to do was wake her up and she would be OK. But when she touched Teresa's arm, she was cold, and J. J. looked at her. It was like looking in a mirror. For the first time, J. J. realized how much they looked alike, and she got so confused.

J. J. didn't know who had died...Teresa or J. J., herself?

Then this loud voice yelled that J. J. should have died instead of Teresa because Teresa was smart, popular, and beautiful, and she deserved to live.

J. J. then looked up and saw all these people sitting in the back of the room, and she saw Teresa's mother yelling at her. It kind of cleared the confusion in her head about who had died. J. J. knew that it was Teresa. Then she passed out. She was asleep or in a coma for three days. She missed Teresa's funeral and became sad, lost, and depressed. She couldn't discuss this with her mother or anyone else. J. J.'s father wasn't home. He was away. There was a rumor that Teresa was her half-sister on her father's side, but it was a taboo topic. No one would discuss it, but everyone would gossip about it.

Zavor said, "You had many close calls in your life. Do you remember now?"

J. J. said, "Yes, I remember...that."

"Due to your close calls, your soul kept on leaving your body. Because we need you in Zonz, we kept on sending your soul back into your body. It was not your time to die yet. Do you understand?"

J. J. said, "Yes...I think I do. But why did you choose to send for me? I mean, why me? Right now."

Zavor said, "J. J., regardless of what you say or how you behave on a conscious level, you have a very good soul. I've dealt with your soul so many times. As a child growing up, you were always helping others more than yourself. Overall, I like it. Take a look at this fundraiser that you participated in, passionately, to help the poor and the sick."

The large screen appeared again. Showing on the screen was a fundraiser for less fortunate children with cancer. In this episode, in front of so many people, on a high-school auditorium stage, J. J. was singing a song. She was so excited, she could not hide it. She was dressed in a long, V-neck dress. Looking like a movie star, she sang her heart out. It was totally Hollywood. She was attracting everyone to come and buy tickets to watch her performance. It was refreshing, lively, and happy. It was touching everyone. They all joined in by moving their hands from side to side. At the end of the show, the crowd gave J. J. a standing ovation.

Zavor said, "There are so many things that I can show you that show me what's in your soul. Your mother rejected you; she wanted a son, not a daughter. She abused you. She constantly hit you and hurt you, and that caused your nightmares. The nightmares continued through your adulthood. Your parents took you from your environment when you were eight years old to another part of Zonz, and then again to another part. Then you went to yet another part. Even with all the different languages and ways of life you had to learn and the rejections and humiliations you had to endure, you always brought joy and helped humans as much as you could. Helping others seems to bring you the most happiness. You are one of the least greedy souls on Zonz, and since keeping you alive on Zonz for us has been somewhat of what you call a 'full-time job,' I feel confident about calling on you. I know you want to change things on Earth and prevent children from being abused by their parents or whoever is raising them. You want everyone to have a better life than you did. That is clear to me. I know you want to change Zonz—Earth—for the better."

J. J. said, "That's all very sweet, but calling on me for *what*?"

Zavor answered, "I want your commitment and dependability for a very special project. You, J. J., will take on this project."

"I'm just an ordinary woman. I'm not able to make a career switch from full-time accounting into full-time real estate. I'm working two jobs to pay my bills. I can't get any sleep. My right leg is shorter than the other, and I don't have a love life or any other life, and you want to depend on me for a special project? *What are you thinking?*" J. J. shouted hysterically.

✳ ✳ ✳

J. J. found herself in the middle of the desert in the middle of the day. It felt like it was at least two hundred degrees. There were lots of lizards running all around her, and she could still hear Zavor's voice.

"You must learn to be calm, J. J."

J. J. woke up in her bed at 3:00 a.m. "Oh my God! Was that a dream, or was it real? Whoa!" It took her a long while to get back to sleep.

CHAPTER SIX

It was Sunday morning. J. J. got out of bed and, in her pajamas and bathrobe, made her way to the kitchen. She caught a glimpse of herself in a mirror. Her hair was all messed up, and she looked half asleep. She walked into the kitchen where Phoebe and Sam were having coffee.

Phoebe looked at J. J. with a smile. "Rough night, J. J.?"

Sam said, "J. J., you got a nice tan! Did you go to one of those tanning places?"

"Ah...what?" J. J. asked, pouring coffee into her cup.

"Yes, the tan looks good on you, J. J.," Phoebe said. "It would look even better if you had your hair combed!"

"Some people wake up in the morning looking like they had a makeup artist and a hair stylist under their bed, but not me! I wake up...au n-a-t-u-r-e-l!" J. J. said.

"Hey, spooky!" Phoebe said and smiled at J. J. "Want some more coffee? I'm coming with you to meet your group today, right, J. J.?"

"Oh, yes...that's today."

J. J. and Phoebe went to the Seaside Café to meet the rest of the group. They got a table.

Alex said, "Hi, J. J."

"Hi, Alex, Danielle, Charles, Ronny. This is my friend Phoebe."

Everyone said hello to Phoebe.

Danielle said, "Barbara will probably be a little late."

The group was sitting in a large round booth. The waitress asked if everyone was ready to order. They all said yes, and they ordered food. George and Barbara arrived and greeted the group.

"Hi, everyone!" Barbara said. "Sorry I'm late. I had to talk to George for a few minutes."

She and George both ordered some food and joined the rest of the group.

George said, "I want to thank everybody for coming to this meeting today. I think it's better to have a group meeting and get to know each other face-to-face and then talk on the phone. I had a chance to talk to Barbara for a few minutes. That was great. This seminar has so many different topics, including the topic of sex, intimacy, and relationships."

Alex said, "I like that one..." and laughed, along with Ronny and Charles.

"Well," George said, "I would like it if we went around the table and each one of you told us about yourself."

Barbara said, "Well, since I'm next to you, George, I will start...I work as a bookkeeper, and I have two kids. Mary is fifteen, and Bobby is eleven. I've been married sixteen years, and my biggest problem is that I'm in an abusive relationship. My husband is very abusive, and I would like to learn how to deal with it. Sometimes, it's really bad, but I have two kids that I have to think about. It scares me to think I couldn't take care of my kids or I could lose my kids. That is pretty much why I'm taking this seminar."

Charles went next. "I'm a medical student, and I'm trying to deal with my parents. They have so many expectations of me that I can't live up to them all. They don't know that I'm gay...I think the truth would really hurt them, you know. My dad is this tough guy, and he expects me to be the same as him. Sometimes, I feel like I'm suffocating because my parents are in my life, and they're very controlling. When do they cut the cord? What hurts me is that I can't be myself with them! I have to hide my feelings and my friends from them. I'm so tired of pretending that

I'm straight! It kills me that I'm supposed to set a good example for my younger brother, and I feel like a failure!"

"I'm a land developer," said Alex. "Well, I took this seminar for the part about sex and intimacy and relationships." He laughed. "Out of curiosity, you know."

Ronny went next. "I sell computers. I'm married and have four boys, fifteen, twelve, ten and eight years old. I would like to better myself, and that's why I took the seminar."

"I am a freelance photographer," said Danielle. "I would like to meet people; that's why I'm here."

It was J. J.'s turn. "In taking this seminar, my goal is to improve my productivity in selling real estate, and I want to find out what is keeping me back."

George said, "I took this seminar, and I got so much out of it—much more than I ever imagined— that I wanted to give something back. That's why I'm coaching. I'm single. I've never been married. By the way, thank you all for sharing. As a group, we will get to know each other well and become good friends. I'm sure we'll help each other. This seminar covers many different topics, and people's humanity and commitment will touch you. You will begin to see life as an opportunity for full self-expression. It is very important to be on time so you don't miss anything. This class will give you a sense of the rich possibilities available to you and a sense of your true power. Miracles shift from being random, inexplicable windfalls to real results—results that are achievable, producible, and even masterable.

"In a way, your life will never be the same. The question becomes one of finding opportunities to expand and master your transformation. It's like turning on the light. And, yes, Alex, sex, intimacy, and relationships are also among the topics." He laughed.

During George's introduction, everyone was served. They had just about finished eating and were now getting ready to leave.

George said, "We have the times scheduled, so you each call me, and we'll discuss whatever you want to change or achieve in your life or whatever, on an individual basis. I will be coaching you." He sipped his coffee.

They all said their good-byes and left the café. J. J. and Phoebe were walking to the car.

Danielle called, "J. J., wait up! I was just wondering if I could talk to you tonight."

J. J. said, "It's OK if you want to call me tonight...or do you want to...talk right now? By the way, great sex lectures the other night!" She smiled and giggled.

Danielle said, "J. J., maybe I could come over? You think?" She looked really pathetic.

J. J. glanced over at Phoebe. "Well, OK...Here is my address." She wrote it on a piece of paper and handed it to Danielle. "Follow my car. I'll drive slowly."

"OK," Danielle said and smiled.

✳ ✳ ✳

J. J., Phoebe, and Danielle arrived at home and entered the kitchen. Phoebe started making coffee, and they all sat down to talk.

Phoebe said, "I'm surprised that you drink coffee, Danielle. You're so young."

J. J. said, "What's up, kid? Spill the beans."

Danielle said, "Well, my parents are driving me crazy. I was renting this place, and my parents had me thrown out so that I could move in with them again. I would rather die! Now, all my stuff is in storage, and I have to find a new place to live! That's a real bitch. I'm so lost...I'm sorry... Does Phoebe live here too?"

Phoebe said, "Yes...I rent a room from J. J."

Danielle said, "Oh, that's perfect. Could I rent a room here too?"

"The only room I have left is the one next to mine, and I use it for painting and sewing," said J. J.

Danielle begged, "Oh please, J. J.! You could still use it if I rented it. Please. I'll pay you in advance—cash. Please, J. J."

Phoebe said, "Oh, come on, J. J. It'll be OK."

"You know I have nightmares sometimes, and I wake up screaming. That's why the room that I rent to Phoebe is way back there, and even then, that far away, sometimes she hears me in the middle of the night. So you don't want to wake up in the middle of the night with me screaming like mad, do you?"

"Oh, I don't mind!" Danielle said, looking pathetic with big, sad eyes. "Please, J.J.?"

J. J. shook her head and looked at Phoebe. Phoebe and Danielle were looking at J. J. with sad eyes.

J. J. said, "Young people like you, Danielle, like to have lots of parties, and I don't go for that."

"No parties, I promise!"

"Oh...OK, Danielle, but no parties. For tonight, you can sleep on the sofa if you like."

Danielle hugged J. J. and danced around with Phoebe. "I'll get my stuff tomorrow. Thanks, J. J.!"

The next day, Phoebe and J. J. arrived home from work, and Danielle was sitting on the sofa.

Phoebe went into the living room. "You know, Danielle, my friend told me that where she works they need a freelance photographer. You already have a job, right?"

Danielle said, "I could use some extra money right now. How much are they paying?"

"I don't know," Phoebe said. "I didn't ask. If you're interested, this is the phone number. Give them a call."

CHAPTER SEVEN

Coach George was talking to Barbara on the phone. George said, "Tell me about the relationship you had with your parents when you were young."

"I got along with my dad just fine, but he was gone most of the time," she said. "He used to protect me from my mom when he was there. My mom used to hit me and pull my hair sometimes...She beat me up, you know, smacked me around. I used to have nightmares of my mother beating me up. Sometimes, I was able to run out before the beating, and she would chase after me until she caught me. Then I was in deep trouble for running away from her. I had so many nightmares. I was so frightened that I would scream most of the night. I still do sometimes. My father used to tell me when I was little when I had those nightmares that I had wings and could fly away to where my mother couldn't catch me. He was trying to help me.

"Sometimes, other people would talk to my mother and say that she should not hit a five-year-old kid, but she didn't stop. Once, the neighbors called the police, and after that, my mother paid this girl much older than me to beat me up in the street, and the girl did. Once when I was so badly hurt, I looked up from the ground where I fell and saw my mother pay the girl money. She told her next time she should do a better job. One time, my parents were fighting so bad that I ran and got onto a bus and sat down. Across from me were this lady and her daughter. The girl kept calling her 'Mom,' and the mother was so sweet to the girl, telling her that she was going to make her favorite dinner and her favorite rice. The lady was holding the girl's hand so sweetly. I never knew of such love before. I wanted some of that love, so I tried to get myself adopted. I told the lady all the things I knew how to do, and I asked her if she wanted to adopt me. She said to stay with her, but later, she took me to my mother and told my mother what I said to her.

"Well, my mother punished me for embarrassing her. She hated me much more than before. I just was not what my mother wanted. Later on, my brother was born, and, oh my God, she loved my brother—her son. She knew how to love him but always rejected me. She always called me stupid."

George said, "You put up with a lot of abuse from your mother and felt that she didn't love you, right?"

Barbara said, "Right. She didn't love me. I was so desperate for a little drop of love."

"For homework, I would like for you to write down all the moods, good and bad. Write down the qualities and the treatments that you got from your mother and another separate list of those from you husband. Bring these two lists to the next class. If your husband gets abusive, please leave the house immediately. Go to your sister's and call me, OK?"

Barbara said, "OK, thanks, George. I'll see you in class."

✳ ✳ ✳

Alex phoned the coach.

"Hi there, Coach!"

George said, "Hi there, Alex. How are you? What's been happening?"

Alex said, "Oh, I'm great. Nothing new going on. I'm looking at the homework, and I'm thinking about how I can design an extraordinary life for myself. Ha, ha."

George said, "Yes, this homework really makes you think. First, let's talk about the way your life is now, and then you can tell me what you would like to change."

"Well, my relationships don't last very long... Let's just say that fidelity is not my strongest suit when it comes to relationships. I was married a long time ago; that lasted three months, and then we divorced. I just like all different women. I don't like to be tied down to just one. You know what I mean, George?"

"If you want to be single and you don't want to be tied down, then why do you want to change that?"

"Well, sometimes I think that I am missing out on something, like the holidays when you can just relax with family, and they all fuss over you, but when you're single, you always have to be on your best behavior. It's hard to relax...Well, you know what I mean. Every time that I get in what might be a meaningful relationship with a woman, I start to look at other women. I get attracted to women very easily, and then infidelity comes in. When the woman that I'm involved with finds out...then it's over. All these women are so jealous. I need some-one who's not so jealous. For me to be with just one lady, it's like eating food without spices, and I love spices and variety. I just can't commit to just one woman."

"Alex, tell me why you took this seminar?"

"Well, it's one of the best places to meet peo-ple who want to invest. I need investors for a new development...I don't know, maybe to learn something about commitment in relationships on the way. Anything is possible, right?"

"So...other than the business part, you have commitment issues? I want to thank you for being honest with me, Alex. Regarding business, I think this is a good place for you to pick up clients and women. But now that you are in this seminar, you have to do homework like everyone else! I would like you to write what's important to you and what is not. What would empower you to take on the challenges of being effective beyond what you had previously imagined possible? Give it to me next class."

"Homework, ha!" said Alex. "Well, OK. Thanks, George. Bye."

✳ ✳ ✳

Danielle called the coach next. "Hello, George. It's me, Danielle."

"Well, hello, Danielle. How are you, darling?"

"I'm fine. Thank you. It's my time to call. I don't really understand the homework."

"Well," said George, "let's just talk for a while. Tell me, how are things with you?"

"Things are OK. I just found a new place to live and a new job. Things are getting better."

"Danielle, let me ask you...This is the same question I ask everyone in the group. Why did you take this seminar? I mean, there must be something that you want out of it, right?"

"Oh, where do I start? Ha, ha, ha! I want to be my own person, and I feel I need help with it.

My parents are so controlling. They are holding and molding me into themselves, so much so that I sometimes feel I'm suffocating, and I need to escape just to survive. I see my parents as so perfect. They don't show any emotion. They are both doctors, and they are always very professional. They love my sister and me, but they never show any emotions or affection. I'm good at photography. I don't want to be a doctor. I don't understand why I can't find a man that I care about. I mean, lots of guys ask me out but not the ones I like...Anyway, are these enough reasons for you, Coach?" She laughed.

George said, "Ha, ha. You know, some people take this seminar just to see what it is about. When I took it, it was to improve myself. I didn't think there was anything in particular, and boy was I surprised! I'm so glad I took it. We all have different reasons. But let me tell you, the results are very surprising to all of us."

Danielle finished her conversation with George and got off the phone.

✳ ✳ ✳

Phoebe said, "Tonight, me, J. J., and Sam are going to rehearse some songs for the benefit next week. Would you like to join us, Danielle? Maybe you can participate in it?"

"I've got a date tonight!" said Danielle. "I've got to change from my jeans into a pretty dress I bought today. He'll be here in five."

There was a knock on the door. Phoebe opened it, and a tall, young, and handsome man was there. He asked for Danielle.

"Hi, Mark," Danielle said. "This is Phoebe, my roommate."
"Hi, Mark!" said Phoebe.

Danielle and Mark left on their date. They went to the restaurant and got a table near the dance floor. After a while, they got up to dance.

CHAPTER EIGHT

Phoebe turned on the TV. There was a car chase in progress. After a long chase, the car turned into a neighborhood, and the driver and passengers disappeared into the neighborhood. The police were searching for them.

J. J. had just finished showing a house to prospective buyers. She locked up the house and walked to her car. It was dark in this isolated area. Just before J. J. reached her car, two men with guns attacked her in the dark. One grabbed her by the arm and dragged her over to a large trash bin. He put a gun to her head. One man told the other man, "This woman is our shield, our ticket out in case the police find us."

J. J. reached into her pocket for something with which to help herself, but the only thing she could find was a thin, bent stick that somehow straightened itself out to about four feet long.

One man said to the other, "Look! She's got a weapon! A little stick?"

Both man laughed at J. J. The stick fell out of J. J.'s hands and floated in the air by itself. The two men tried to knock the stick down, but they were unable to do it. One man was still holding onto J. J.'s arm and had a bunch of her hair in his grip. While the other man was occupied with the stick, the man holding J. J. was watching out for the police. The stick suddenly opened up and formed a circle like a vortex. Suddenly, the stick sucked the two men into the center. They spun like Frisbees. As they tried to get out, they let go of J. J. and got sucked right into the hole. They were both screaming and yelling. The round hole turned into the stick again and disappeared into thin air in the dark place.

The police were searching the area and heard some screaming and yelling. J. J. was getting up from her fall to the floor. Just as she was dusting herself off, her hair messed up and her clothes ripped at the shoulder, the police arrived, searching for the two men. They had seen the men in this area and followed them. They asked J. J. what had happened.

"There were two men who attacked me and held a gun to my head. Then somehow, they just disappeared. I'm not sure how, but they disappeared. I didn't get a good look at them. It was dark, and it happened so fast!"

The police asked J. J. if she was OK. J. J. assured them she was. J. J. told the police again that she didn't get a good look at the two men's faces because it was so dark and they had come from behind her. Finally, the police escorted J. J. to her car and made sure she was safe.

J. J. drove away, and the police continued their search for the two men.

J. J. was so glad she had taken—or stolen— the stick from her unexplainable dreams. That left J. J. wondering about the stick, her dreams, and the two men who had been sucked into the vacuum that had been made by the stick. She was so puzzled. J. J. was shaking but decided to go to class and think about all of it later.

At the seminar, the class started, and Alex greeted J. J. and Danielle. They all walked in and sat down next to each other.

✳ ✳ ✳

At Barbara's house, her husband was detaining her, trying to prevent her from attending the seminar. He was holding on and hurting her arm.

"Please let me go. Stop hurting me. I'll be back as soon as it's over."

She finally broke loose and left, and even though she rushed, Barbara arrived at the seminar late. In the hallway, just before entering the large double doors, she was lectured by one of the seminar's assistants about being late.

"It's not like I wanted to be late," Barbara said.

The assistant said, "Remember your commitment to being on time."

Barbara entered through the double doors and found a seat. The seminar was in progress, and a pretty young lady was standing up and sharing.

Michelle, the young lady, said, "I know that people at my workplace talk behind my back. It is very uncomfortable for me. It happens every day, and it makes me feel paranoid. It's kind of embarrassing. I am confident, but this is so conspicuous. Four to five people stand around staring at me, talking. As soon as I pass by, they stop talking and just stare at me. After a while, it gets to you. I don't know if I should look for another job or not."

Michael asked, "What do you think they're saying behind your back?"

"They stare and make fun of the way I look, and I think they talk about the way I talk and walk and the way I wear my clothes. They look at me like they hate me. They never talk to me. They talk *about* me, and that makes me very uncomfortable every day! I have to work there, so it makes my life hard. It sounds stupid, but this is the way I live my everyday life!"

Michael said, "Well, is it OK if I ask some people in this class what they're thinking about you when they look at you?"

"OK," she said.

"What do the people in your job look like? Choose some of the people in this classroom, and those chosen please come up in front of the classroom."

Michelle pointed out five people, mostly men, and they came up in front of the classroom.

Michael said, "We are going to reenact what goes on in your place of work. Now, Michelle, here they are. This is your chance to ask them why they're staring, what they're talking about when staring at you, why they hate you—ask them whatever you like."

"Why do you stare at me like I am a piece of meat?" She pointed to a man named Russ.

"I look at you because you're pretty, not because you're a piece of meat," said Russ. "I think you look very nice. If I worked with you, I would want to get to know you."

Michelle pointed at James next. "I see you giving me dirty looks like you hate me. Why?"

James said, "How can I hate you? I don't even know you? These are not dirty looks. I'm a little nearsighted. I'm sorry you don't like the way I look at you, but it has nothing to do with you."

Michelle asked similar questions of the others, and they all gave positive answers.

Michael asked them, "Are you trying to be nice, people?"

All those whom Michelle had chosen said that they were not.

"Michelle, this is about you, not about anyone else," Michael explained. "It's what you make it mean! There is no way you could know what anyone is thinking! Maybe you could say hello to your co-workers and break the ice...get them to talk to you. But remember to take things at face value. Don't make it mean anything. How do you feel now, Michelle?"

Michelle said, "I feel relieved!" She laughed. "I find it very therapeutic to talk about it. I will say hello to my co-workers. Yeah, I can understand now."

Michael asked, "Who else feels the way Michelle does?"

Half of the class raised their hands.

"You're not alone in this, Michelle. Many of us feel that way too at one time or another, but try what I said, and let us know how it turns out.

Michael addressed the whole group again. "Who else wants to share? Come up in front of the classroom."

Leiden, an African-American woman, stood up. "I'm a schoolteacher, and I have one student who drives me crazy. I guess there is always one in every group. She's got such a mouth on her. I spoke to her parents two times, but it didn't help. It made things worse; she's so sarcastic."

Michael said, "Well, let's start with you. What if you take a stand that surpasses what was previously possible and exhibit performance that defies old limits and territory? You've got to understand where *you* are coming from first. Do you like teaching?"

"Yes...absolutely, I love teaching. All the other students like me."

"Then teaching, for you, comes from the heart? Answering her questions and teaching her, it's what you love to do? That's all very positive no matter what or how she talks to you. Just because she has a problem, it doesn't mean that you have a problem also. After all, you are the intelligent teacher, and you must always remain positive. If she chooses to remain negative, that's up to her. Just remember where you're coming from, OK? Anyone else want to share?"

A lady named Julie came forward. "I worked on my homework and also discussed this issue with my coach last week. I read the assignment on sex, intimacy, and relationships. I was interested in the part on how sexual love, or what is sexy to one's mind, comes from when we were very young, when sex first originated in our minds—what we as humans first learned or first thought was sexy to us. I'm in the middle of a divorce, and I was having a hard time understanding why my husband had been cheating on me for a long time and why he denied it every time, even though he was caught in the act. Basically, most men will marry someone they think is going to take care of them in life, like a mother figure, but they will sneak out to have sex with the one who fits their vision or has the characteristics of the one who represents sexy in their minds, like the first thought of what was sexy that originated in their subconscious mind...That's the one they'll sneak out and have sex with. Apparently, I was the one who took care of him, like a mother, I guess, and he went out and found someone who was the vision of what's sexy to him. It's a very important subject to learn. If I'd known this before, it would have saved me so much time and trouble, not to mention all the heartache."

Michael said, "The subconscious mind is very powerful in driving us through life. It's so important to understand our own actions so that we can better our lives. There are all different kinds of love—parent-child love, sibling love, sexual love. When and how it originated in our mind is different for each one of us, depending on our environment or what we were exposed to at that time in our lives. And it will drive us through our lives. So, yes, when we choose a sexual partner, it is someone who resembles in looks, characteristics, and personality the one whom our childhood memory associates with the moment that the idea of sexual love first originated in our mind. It goes back to that and drives us through life. That is why sexy means different things to different people. I think before people get serious about getting married, they should learn all about each other and communicate so that when they do get married, they at least know somewhat of their sexual expectations. We will start working on this subject next week. Thank you all for sharing. Let's form groups."

The separate groups all formed together. Alex, Danielle, Barbara, Ronny, Charles, J. J., and George formed a circle with chairs and started sharing.

George said, "Hi, everybody..." Barbara handed George a piece of paper, and he could see an angry bruise on her wrist. "Barbara, what happened to your wrist?"

"My husband didn't want me to come tonight." She took a deep breath.

George said, "Barbara, would you like to talk in private about this, or are you OK talking to the group?"

Barbara said, "That's OK. I think the group already knows."

"Why do you let your husband abuse you like this?" George asked.

"Sometimes, he's so nice. He's a good man, but he has a bad temper. And we have two kids, you know. They need their father."

"Barbara, no one has the right to abuse you! Just think what your kids are learning from this.

Usually, this kind of abuse results in such violence that some women get killed. Then what's going to happen to your kids? You can't help your kids if you're dead! It all starts small. What's keeping him from beating them up? Especially if you're not there! I know it takes courage, and you know that I'm here for you," said George.

The group assured her they were there for her too.

Barbara said, "It's not that easy, you know."

George said, "What would it take for you to take your kids and leave your husband?"

"I have to find an apartment first, or I could stay with my sister."

George said, "I'm going to keep tabs on you. I will read your homework, and we will continue this conversation over the phone. Will you be OK?"

"Oh yeah. This is nothing new. It's been going on for a long time now. I will call you on the phone, Coach."

Ronny said, "My wife and I are having trouble, too! It's mostly about money. I took this seminar to improve my sales. I hope it works. I'm investing my savings to improve myself so that I can be a better provider for my family. My wife complains all the time. She stays home with the four kids. Now that the kids are older, I wish she would find a job! Instead, she sits home looking messy all the time and complaining that I don't bring home enough money!"

George said, "J. J. wants to improve her sales also. Right, J. J.?"

"Yes! That's my goal!"

Alex said, "I would buy anything from J. J. if she smiled at me."

J. J. jokingly gave him the evil eye.

George said, "What about you, Charles? How are you doing? You look kind of pale today."

Charles said, "I'm just burned out from my studies. I have a final coming up. My father wants me to go fishing with him. If I go, he's going to try to toughen me up, like usual, so I'm not going. I think I'm tough enough."

"And you, Danielle?" said George. "How are things? You're so quiet tonight!"

"I'm OK! I'll call you tomorrow morning, George. Is that OK?"

"Next week, we'll be discussing the subject of love, intimacy, and relationships, so be prepared," said George. "For homework, I want you to think about when and where thoughts of love first originated in your mind—any kind of love, including sexual love, brother and sister love, parental love...Good night! See you all next week."

Everyone started getting ready to leave, scheduling times to call the coach, and walking to the parking lot. Alex tried to flirt with J. J., but she was too cool.

✳ ✳ ✳

Danielle and J. J. arrived home, and Phoebe was waiting for them with coffee and tea.

"Hi, you two!"

"The coach was right about you being so quiet tonight, Danielle!" said J. J.

"Danielle *quiet*?" exclaimed Phoebe. "Oh, let me feel your forehead! Are you sick?"

"Noooo...Phoebe, did Mark call tonight?"

"No...not Mark. You have some other calls! How did the date go last night with Mark? Did you two have fun?"

"Yes, we did! We had a nice time. Most of the time, when I meet someone like Mark, someone who's financially secure, comes from a well-to-do family, and has such a nice personality, I just blow him off! I don't know why I do that...I just do. I alienate men like Mark kind of subconsciously! You know! The guys who are jerks I try real hard with, and then I complain that I only meet jerks. That's why I don't have any relationships."

"I wonder what makes men cheat," said Phoebe.

"In class, this lady, Julie, shared that she just put all the pieces together about why her husband cheated in their marriage," said J. J. "She felt like she had just figured it all out. The leader was asking us to think about when love first originated, and there's so many kinds of love—like parent-child love, sibling love, sexual love, and so on. When and how did the idea of sexual love originate in your mind? It starts when we are children, and it's different for each of us, like, for instance, Julie shared that her husband has two older sisters. The oldest is Mary, and the second, Angie. His mother was sick, and Mary took care of her younger brother, later Julie's husband, looking after him. She fed him and made sure he had clothes. She got him out of trouble, the whole thing. Angie was always sneaking around kissing her boyfriend and got pregnant at seventeen. She got married and left the house. Then David married Julie. She looked like his sister Mary, who had taken care of him when he was little. Most men want to marry a woman who's going to take care of them. David fooled around and cheated with women who looked like and had the same characteristics as his sister Angie. In David's mind, Angie's behaviors and actions represented sexual love. That was how that idea originated in his mind when he was little. He would only find women like Angie sexy, and that's why he cheated most of the time without knowing it. It's all in his subconscious mind. Well, he knew he was cheating!"

J. J. continued, "Michael is right, you know! It's true, everything that happened to us when we were growing up, all the way into our teens. Whatever happened, we all gave meaning to it. And because we were so young, we took it to be so real that it goes into our subconscious minds and drives us through our adult lives, or until we go back to that happening, relive it all over again, and give it a different meaning from an adult's point of view. That enables us to sort of disable the buttons that control us—subconsciously speaking. Even after you have done that, you still have to learn to distinguish. When that button lights up again, remember the new meaning you gave that button, and defuse it."

Danielle said, "So you mean the reason for this behavior comes from my childhood?"

"Oh yes, Danielle! I'm sure of it! As adults, we don't take things so seriously, but as kids, we took everything as gospel! Everything our parents said and did was also the gospel. Kids are all alike. That's why the homework for the seminar is very important! It allows you to get to your subconscious mind and get rid of the past, which controls and drives us in a way we don't want to go—like being nice to jerks and alienating guys like Mark! It doesn't seem to be your cup of tea, but you do it!"

Danielle said, "Hmm...yeah, I'm starting to get it. Now we have the subject of love, intimacy, and relationships for homework to think about...Hey, J. J., changing the subject here, do you like Alex?"

Phoebe said, "Hmm...Alex is so cute! He likes J. J." She smiled.

"Alex is a flirt!" J. J. said. "He's nice as a friend! But that is it."

Danielle said, "Alex flirts with every woman he sees. He told me that he has a girlfriend and that she's the love of his life, and yet he flirts with every woman he meets! And he brags about it too...I saw him flirting...well, kissing passionately with this blonde in the hallway before the seminar started. I don't like guys like that, you know? I mean he's a nice friend from the group, but that's about it. I'm glad that you don't *like him* like him, J. J.!"

Phoebe said, "When we were in the restaurant, he made a pass at me! He sat next to me, and he was flirting with me. I just didn't make anything of it, but he tried. He must think he's hot stuff because he's a developer!"

Late in the afternoon, J. J. was in her shorts and tank top and barefoot in her art room, working on her latest painting. She was surrounded by easels holding oil paintings, and each canvas was painted with a different scene. The music was on, and J. J. was dancing, singing, and twirling, living in the music and painting. A breeze came in from the open windows. Sometimes, J. J. slid from one side of the room to the other while dancing; it was quite a show. This was a tension release for J. J. She got lost in her art. J.J. was very passionate about her art.

Danielle and Alex walked in on her.

Alex said, "Hi, gorgeous! You look like an eighteen-year-old chick!"

J. J. was surprised. "Oh...hi! How long have you been watching me? I didn't know you were there."

Danielle said, "Alex came over to get the homework assignment."

She took Alex into the living room and gave him a piece of paper. "Here's the homework!"

Alex flirted with Danielle. "Want to go for coffee, Danielle?"

Danielle declined. "Thanks, Alex, but I have a boyfriend, and we're going out tonight."

Alex said, "Bye, Danielle." He went back into the room where J. J. was painting. "Bye, J. J.!"

J. J. and Danielle said, "Bye, Alex!"

Alex finally left.

Danielle walked up to J. J. "I had to tell him that I have a boyfriend so that he would leave me alone. He came all the way here to get the homework? He could have called, and I would have told him! I don't think he missed hearing that the homework is on the subject of sex, intimacy, and relationships!"

CHAPTER NINE

That night, J. J. had another dream about Crystal Planet.

J. J. saw a big, strong guard and found herself talking to him. "Hi! I'm J. J....and what's your name?"

The guard responded, "Zacorian, that's my name."

"Hi, Zacorian! You know, I have so many questions about this place. Is this all about Egypt? There're so many Egyptians here all around."

"No!"

"Well, you seem very nice. I'd like to talk to you and ask you some questions. Is that OK?"

"Yes!"

"Oh—thank you. Well, I'm glad that you're here right now. I'm not too crazy about Zavor. He sent me to the desert last time. Actually, I think he's delusional!"

Zacorian asked, "Don't you like Zavor?"

"Well, I like him from a distance. You know, the way you like the sun...so you don't get burned!"

Just then, J. J. turned her head slightly to one side, and her eyes caught a glimpse of Zavor, who was suddenly standing behind her. He had heard the conversation.

J. J. found herself in the hot desert again, surrounded by lizards, scorpions, and other crawling creatures in the hot, steaming sun. "Oops! Oh... no..." She gasped for air and took a deep breath. "Here, lizard, lizard, lizard!" She looked around. "Oh, well, here I am *again*! Well, last time I was here, I woke up later at home. I guess I will do the same now. Later, I'll wake up in my bed safe and sound, so I might as well get a tan...I'll wake up in a little while! So, ha, ha."

✳ ✳ ✳

J. J. woke up and slowly opened her eyes. She found herself lying on a flat bed shaped like a large half egg with a purple light shining on her and a hunk of a man—big, broad shoulders, and about six feet tall with piercing eyes—standing by her side looking at her.

"Hello, J. J. I am Vyzier!" he said.

J. J. looked like a scarecrow—lifeless, very sick, and unable to get up or move much. She was totally disoriented and unaware of being on Crystal Planet.

"Vyzier? Who are you?"

"Well, I used to be a comedian, but now I practice medicine...I'm your doctor!" he said jokingly, with a devious smile and somewhat of a wise-guy attitude. "And I am taking care of you. I'm going to—"

J. J. interrupted him, her eyes popping out of her head. "A doctor with a sense of humor? And you're going to *practice* on me? Oh...*no...no...no!*" She waved her hands and shook her head in fear of him.

Vyzier said, "I will help you take a little walk, just a few steps at a time. I know you're tense...Just relax. Don't be frightened! I don't bite humans! Not unless I'm very hungry...Ha, ha!" He lifted J. J. and helped her stand up.

"Where am I?" she asked. She was still unable to walk on her own.

Vyzier said, "You are in Bingonium Place...on Crystal Planet, recovering."

"Recovering! From what?"

"Your brain *fried* in the desert. You almost died from severe burns, J. J. But you're doing much better now under the circumstances."

"How long have I been here?"

"Two weeks now."

"Two weeks! Oh my God! I have to work and pay my bills! I have so many things to do!"

"Your condition would have been fatal on Zonz. Your fate is to stay alive. You've been undoubtedly selected for a special project, for reasons I cannot fathom at this time, and Zavor is like...your teacher."

"Teacher! Oh...nooo...I'm in trouble now!" She shook her head, trying to get her breath.

"Don't sweat the small stuff, J. J.," Vyzier said. "Besides, we sent your clone to Zonz to do your work for you." Vyzier was holding J. J. up, getting her to take a few steps.

"A clone? Of me? You sent a clone to Earth—Zonz? Will she be able to do my work? That Bingonium man—*Zavor*—tried to kill me! Teacher...hmm."

"Yes, J. J. Your audacity with Zavor is not good! Never underestimate his authority. Why do you hate him?"

"I don't understand why he wants to keep me alive! He put me in the desert and left me there to die? How would you like to be sort of kidnapped in your dreams and be put in a position so that fear eats you alive? You don't know if next time you'll wake up or whether you're going to catch your breath or not. I don't hate him...I hate the invasion in my life! I feel like I'm losing my mind!" She tried to catch her breath.

"The road to righteousness through the methods of discipline is advised—although it might seem damnably difficult at the moment."

J. J., looking half dead, gave him a side look as she took a deep breath.

"I'm going to need a dictionary to understand what you're saying!"

J. J. suddenly lost consciousness. Her frail condition worsened. Vyzier was very concerned and looked worried. He carried J. J. in his arms back to bed. He held her in his arms and kissed her face.

"J. J., you must come back...I want you to come back. Don't go, J. J.!" he begged.

Vyzier, still holding J. J. in his arms and warming her now cold body, took her to the large, round, crystal box. Vyzier came back out of the crystal box with J. J. in his arms. He put her back on the oval bed.

Holding her hand and touching her face, he looked at her very lovingly. J. J. seemed to come back to life. She slowly opened her eyes, and the first thing she saw was Vyzier, who was looking at her adoringly. His loving gaze spoke volumes. Vyzier's facial expression told her he was very happy she had opened her eyes. J. J. looked at Vyzier and started to realize that maybe this was not the first time that Vyzier had attended to her after a near-death experience.

In a very faint and soft voice, she asked, "Can I...ask you a question, Vyzier?"

Vyzier agreed loudly and followed it up with a big smile. "You can have gold coins if you want! *Yes*...anything."

"How many times have you...ah...when did you start to...help me with my...near-death experiences...or my...death experiences?"

Vyzier lowered his voice. "From the start."

"You're the one who keeps on putting me...back together again?"

"At the beginning, I was assigned to help you, like you said, put you back together...ha, ha! Later on...I volunteered!"

J. J. smiled at first but then was very moved. "Were you a doctor then or a comedian?"

"I was undecided then." He smiled. "Look, J. J., I have a present for you!"

J. J. was still unable to move. "What is it? Tell me!"

Vyzier had a big smile on his face. "It's a dictionary!"

J. J. smiled back at him. "A dictionary? Just what I needed."

✳ ✳ ✳

Back home on Zonz (Earth), in the kitchen of J. J.'s house, Phoebe and Danielle were having coffee. J. J.'s clone came in and sat down.

Phoebe said, "J. J., did you finally get the hairdresser and makeup artist under your bed? This past couple of weeks, you've looked great so early in the morning. Your hair is all in place, and it looks just perfect!" Phoebe smiled to let J. J. know she was joking.

Danielle said, "J. J., the bookstore called. They got your book in."

J. J.'s clone replied, "Thanks, Danielle. I will get it this afternoon." She closed her briefcase and rushed out. "I don't want to be late for work!"

✳ ✳ ✳

Later that afternoon, in front of the Coffee Bean restaurant, J. J.'s clone was sitting outside at a small table, sipping coffee, and reading her new book. An attractive, well-dressed, and very refined man approached her.

"Excuse me, is this seat taken?"

J. J.'s clone said, "No, it's not!"

The man put his large cup of coffee on the small table and accidentally spilled it all over J. J.'s new book and her lap.

"Oh—I'm so sorry! I'm so terribly sorry!" said the man.

With some napkins, he began wiping J. J.'s lap and book. It looked like the spilled coffee was staining J. J.'s slacks.

J. J.'s clone said, "Ouch! Hooooo!" She stood up and began wiping off the coffee with napkins.

"Please accept my apologies," the man said. "My clumsiness is unforgivable."

J. J.'s clone said, "Oh...I'll live. It's OK; don't worry." She smiled.

"My name is Sid Silverman," the man said. "Here is my business card, and this is me." He handed J. J.'s clone his driver's license. "I don't want you to think I'm some kind of nut!"

J. J.'s clone said, "I don't want your driver's license. I will keep your business card." She smiled and handed him his driver's license back.

Sid said, "I want to pay for your slacks and your book. They're both ruined."

"Don't worry about it! The stain will come off, and the book will dry."

"Then I will come back here tomorrow with a new book for you. What's the name of your book?" He wrote down the name of the book on a piece of paper. "I'd like to come back and meet you here tomorrow, same place, same time? Oh, please, let me at least do this!"

J. J.'s clone said, "You really don't have to!"

Sid said, "Oh, I insist. I didn't get your name."

"My name is J. J. Well, I have to go. I'll see you tomorrow then."

Sid said, "I'll see you tomorrow, J. J."

Sid's face was red, and he looked kind of smitten with J. J.

✳ ✳ ✳

Just as Danielle walked in, the phone rang. It was Alex, asking her out.

"Hi, Alex...No, not tonight. I'm going out with my boyfriend...Yes, everything is going well...Yes, George is a good coach. I'm getting ready to go out...Just out....J. J. went to get her book at the bookstore near the Coffee Bean...OK, bye."

✳ ✳ ✳

Alex walked into a restaurant and met a tall brunette.

"Hi, Lynn! Are you alone? Why don't you join me?"

Lynn said, "Well, OK, Alex," with a big smile. They sat down very close to each other. Lynn was about forty-two years old. "I always see you at the seminar with Danielle. Is she your girlfriend?"

"Well, no...Danielle likes me, but no." His ego was huge.

They flirted for a bit. Alex's smile sent a sudden jolt through Lynn's chest. She was fascinated. Her gaze lingered on his lips and then rose to meet his eyes. There was no stopping him from kissing her passionately after that. Alex suggested continuing this pleasure at her place. The thought sent delicious shivers down her spine. They left, holding hands and staring into each other's eyes.

They entered her place.

Alex said, "You are more beautiful than any woman I've known." He touched her arms up and down. Her eager expression held the hunger of a cat about to pounce. They undressed each other and got into bed and under the covers, where the passion of lovemaking became very intense.

✳ ✳ ✳

In the living room of J. J.'s house, J. J.'s clone, Danielle, Sam, and Phoebe were sitting around in their pajamas.

Phoebe said, "It's been a long time since I had a slumber party! Ha, ha!"

They were playing their favorite music and mimicking the songs, taking turns being the lead singer. J. J.'s clone liked to mimic Diana Ross. On top of the coffee table, using a hairbrush as a microphone, she sang. The other three ladies were the Supremes. They all laughed and played like teenagers. After lots of singing and dancing, they got down and started talking about their dreams and goals.

Danielle said, "I've always wanted to be a bride. I don't know if that will ever happen. I'm getting old now."

Phoebe smacked Danielle on the head with a pillow. "You! Old! Ha, ha, ha!"

The others joined in, and the pillow fight began. Feathers flew all over the room. J. J.'s clone used a white towel as a veil and put a plastic flowerpot on top of Danielle's head.

"Here comes the bride, tan-tan-ta-da," she sang.

Sam gave the plastic flowers to Danielle. "Throw the bouquet! Throw it to me!" she commanded.

Danielle strolled around the living room like a bride and finally threw the bouquet behind her. The others all tried to catch it.

✳ ✳ ✳

The next day at the Coffee Bean, sitting outside, Sid waited for J. J. When J. J.'s clone arrived, Sid was fixing his suit jacket. He greeted J. J.'s clone, who looked stunning in her two-piece black-and-white suit.

Sid said, "Hi, J. J.! You look great! How are you?"

"I'm fine, thanks, and you?" the clone said.

"I'm great. Here is your new book, no stains... ha, ha. I like this book. It's very interesting...I've got lots of questions about it. Maybe you could have dinner with me and answer some of them for me." He smiled.

"Thanks, but I can't tonight."

"Well then, tomorrow night? Ha...before you say no, I know some of the finest restaurants in town and nightclubs, if you like dancing or just listening to some great music..."

"I'll have to get back to you on that," she said. "I'll call you tonight."

"J. J., I've got to show you this," Sid said.

Next door was a flower shop, and Sid put his arm around J. J.'s clone's shoulders and walked in to show her a beautiful basket of flowers.

"Do you like these flowers, J. J.?"

"They are absolutely beautiful."

"They're yours!" he said. "They remind me of you...beautiful."

Sid paid for the flowers.

"Thank you! How nice!"

Sid carried the flowers for her to the car, and J. J.'s clone drove away.

"I shall await your call. Take care, J. J. Bye," Sid said to the retreating car.

✳ ✳ ✳

Phoebe said, "It's Sunday morning. Are you going to call Sid? J. J., look at these beautiful flowers! He must really like you!"

J. J.'s clone called Sid. "Hi, Sid. I can't make it tonight. This coming Saturday? Well, OK. About seven? Yes, you can call me. We'll talk during the week...Bye!"

Danielle asked, "J. J., you're not doing anything tonight, are you?" She smiled.

"Yes...my hair and my nails, and I'll wash my clothes, pay my bills. Why do you ask?"

Phoebe said, "She's just playing hard to get with Sid, aren't you, J. J.? I would have gone and had a good time, but J. J. is a 'Rules' girl...Ha, ha! She goes by *The Rules* book!"

"Men love to conquer," J. J. said. "If you surrender yourself to them, then they have nothing to conquer. You ruin their hunt, their pursuit, their pleasure. I'm not playing hard to get. I'm just giving Sid something to conquer. Besides, I do have other things to do...I'm working today."

Danielle said, "Can I borrow *The Rules* book? Who has it? I'm having dinner with my co-workers tonight! I need this book!"

They all laughed.

* * *

That Monday at noon, Barbara was at her workplace. Her husband, Carl, showed up unexpectedly to take her out to lunch. While he was waiting for her, he flirted heavily with Barbara's co-worker, Beth. Even though Beth was engaged, she flirted back. When Barbara arrived, ready to go to lunch, Carl was still flirting with Beth and touching himself on his private parts in front of Barbara while everyone else was looking on.

As they walked to lunch, Barbara suddenly burst into tears. She was unable to control herself.

Carl asked, "Why are you crying? Honey?"

Barbara said, "Beth is engaged, you know? Why are you flirting with her in front of me? And people in my office?"

Carl said, "Oh just leave me alone. You're crazy...you're so jealous. You're crazy...oh man!"

Back at Barbara's office, the group of people who worked with Barbara were all talking about Carl and laughing at Barbara. But as soon as she walked in, they all went quiet.

When Barbara arrived home, she found a girl coming out of her back door. The girl appeared to be about nineteen years old. Barbara thought she lived in the front unit. She walked in, and Carl was just zipping up his pants. Barbara knew what had been going on.

Barbara asked, "What did that girl want? What was she doing here?"

Carl said, "Oh what? More jealousy? You are so screwed up, you know? I don't have to answer you! What? You're jealous again? Where is my dinner?"

"I just asked you a question. What did she want?"

Carl said, "Nothing...I don't know. You know, you're driving me crazy with your jealousy. None of your business, you understand? Gee! Look at you nag, nag, nag." He grabbed her by the arm and pushed her. Barbara fell to the ground.

"You're not making any sense," she said, trying to sit up. She was so upset that she lost her breath and slumped to the floor again.

Carl said, "Look at you, trying to get attention from me—ha, I'm not falling for that." He kicked her in the ribs while she was still on the floor. "Get up, you crazy thing. Your whole family is crazy. You're all nuts!"

The kids walked in, and the son ran to help Barbara up. The daughter got her a glass of water. Both were scared. Barbara looked ill, holding her side near her ribs where Carl had kicked her.

Carl said, "Look at her; she's so emotional. She's trying to make a scene. Oh, what a bitch! She's trying to make me look bad!" He had a violent expression on his face. The phone rang.

"Answer the phone, Barbara!"

Barbara, still curled up, answered the phone. "Hello...Oh hi, George!" Her voice was trembling. "This is a bad time to talk. Can I call you back? Yeah, I'm OK. I'll call you later."

Carl said, "Who's George? Your boyfriend?" He became more violent.

"He's from the seminar! He's my coach. It's about my homework," she said pleadingly.

"Those people are screwing with your head. You better not tell them anything about me! *You understand*?" he shouted viciously. "Add this to your jealousy. I had sex with the next-door neighbor. Yes, that's right! Beckie, the skinny, ugly bitch who tells everybody she's happily married. She likes having sex with me. Actually, she's been chasing me for some time now. I don't even like her! Yes, I did it. I had sex with her just to humiliate you!"

Barbara got away from Carl. The phone rang, and Carl answered. After he had a confidential discussion on the phone, he left the house. This gave Barbara a chance to get the two kids into her car. She drove to her sister's. She called George for a meeting so they could talk without interruption.

Barbara met George in a coffee shop. "Hi, Coach! Thanks for coming. I really need some help before something happens to my kids. You never know what mood my husband is going to be in. I'm so glad I have you to talk to about this mess, Coach."

"Well, thank you for trusting me with this situation," said George. "I know this is really hard for you, and I am trying to help you. I checked your homework paper where you compared your husband to your mother, and I can clearly see that they both have the same characteristics, and they both abused you. You once told me that you felt your mother never loved you. As human beings, we all need love from our parents, and when we don't get it, we try to get it from someone who has the same characteristics as our parents. It could be a mother or a father—it doesn't matter. So you took the abuse to get the love through Carl that you wanted from your mother. Many people do that, but the right way is to go directly to the source: the parent. If the parent is dead, write him or her a letter and explain how you feel. In your case, you could just talk to your mother. Does this make sense to you?"

"Yes...it does! I realize that the way Carl treats me is not love. He gets what he can out of me. I remember once, well, recently, my mother told me that she liked my hair and that I looked nice. That's a drop of love. I really didn't understand it before, but I do now. I don't know how I stayed with Carl all that time. I talked to my sister, and she's going to let us stay with her until I get my own place. The kids are happy to be out and away from Carl. I can't believe what I was doing to my kids!" Barbara began crying. "Coach, you opened up my eyes today. I can't thank you enough. I'm going to call an attorney and file for divorce. I hope I have the courage to follow through with it."

George said, "This is a major breakthrough for you, Barbara. I know you have the courage to follow through. You are much smarter than you give yourself credit for, and I know you're strong. Understanding this situation is the most important step. Learn to nurture, love, and guide the child in you. And you know I'm here for you anytime."

✳ ✳ ✳

In J. J.'s house, J. J.'s clone, Phoebe, and Danielle were sitting in the kitchen booth when Sam came in.

Sam said, "Well, my parents' living trust has been settled, and with my share and my brother's share, we're going to open up a coffeehouse around the corner! Oh, I'm so happy. It'll be a lot of work at the beginning, and I know that, but we'll have something to our name that we can say is ours!"

Phoebe said, "Congratulations! I'm glad you guys stopped fighting over the money!"

"It's incredible how we fought over that money!" said Sam. "I thought it would take forever to settle the whole thing, so much money went to the lawyers...Oh what a mess...but it's over now."

Danielle said, "When is the coffeehouse going to open?"

"Well, Phoebe is the interior decorator we're going to hire...so..."

"Oh, thanks! I'll be happy to do it! You know working in the hotel as head caterer, it pays OK, but I can always use some extra money!"

J. J.'s clone said, "I'm happy for you, Sam. Phoebe is a great interior decorator. You're going to be happy, Sam. You'll see."

Danielle said, "When were you an interior decorator, Phoebe?"

"My partner and I had this interior decorating business together, and it was very good until my partner, Pete, stole all the money and left me broke. So I got out of the business. It was so hard to take. I'm over Pete now. I had this offer for a catering position, and I took it. Don't ever trust men! Greed is their business."

Danielle said, "My mother says to be happy with a man, you must understand him a lot and love him a little."

J. J.'s clone said, "We got a smart one here, ha, ha!" She hugged Danielle.

The phone rang.

Danielle said, "Hello...hi, Alex..."

The other ladies started laughing when they heard the name Alex.

Phoebe said, "Speak of the devil! Ha, ha!"

CHAPTER TEN

B ack in Bingonium Place on Crystal Planet, in a bed made of crystal that looked like a large half egg floating in the air, with a soft white mattress and cushions for a pillow, was J. J., a purple light shining on her. She was looking very pale, and she was much skinnier than her clone on Earth. She was talking to Vyzier.

Vyzier said, "J. J., what would make you feel better? What would you like to do for fun?"

"Well..." She smiled. "I would like to ride with you in a rocket ship through the universe listening to rock-and-roll music, like Elvis Presley's song 'Don't Be Cruel' or something like that..."

Vyzier said, "All right then, let's go!"

"What? Really? Ha, ha! Oh, really!" she gushed.

J. J.'s condition was still fragile, so Vyzier helped her up and carried her in his arms to a dark corner, and out into the universe they went in a small rocket ship with the music playing loudly.

"Don't be cruel, to a heart that's true."

They passed some very beautiful colors and breathtaking lights in the Andromeda galaxy, or was it the Milky Way? J. J. was holding onto Vyzier, her arms around him, because she was afraid of heights. She started to have butterfly feelings, and those feelings were starting to grow. Her heart was beating faster. She found comfort in holding onto him. Suddenly, an explosion seemed to come from a projectile directed at them. They jetted away fast and far, but the explosions followed them. The enemy was following closer and closer, shooting at them. They were traveling as fast as possible, but the enemy got really close. Vyzier shot a large, round glass (like a small flying saucer) at the enemy, and it seemed to vacuum the enemy into it and send it through space.

Vyzier and J. J. found themselves on a new, dark planet and were somewhat lost. On this dark planet, thunder rumbled, and lightning sparked all the way to the horizon. It seemed like this planet was charged up with electricity, and the power was totally on overload. They could not stop, or they'd be totally fried. Soon, sparkling stars came to their rescue. The stars surrounded them and guided them out. At the time, the dark planet's soil was like dust or sand. A huge hole formed. Out of the center of this hole, something like a tornado of dust or sand blew out fiercely, blinding and hitting them and all other passing vessels. With its strong, spinning vacuum suction, it swallowed the other vessels and almost swallowed them as well.

The stars that came to their rescue formed a spinning suction and pulled them out, preventing them from being vacuumed in and swallowed by this mysterious sandy hole on this hostile dark planet with its frying hot atmosphere. They were guided out by the stars, but just when they thought they were safe, they were attacked again. They were still on the dark planet. This attack was more aggressive than the first one. J. J. didn't know the first thing about the instruments in the rocket ship and had no way to defend herself. She knew making the wrong decision could be disastrous for both of them. After a brief hesitation, she decided to help by asking Vyzier which button to push. Vyzier was fighting for their lives. He pointed to the button for J. J. to push. Vyzier and J. J. were intensely fighting the enemy together. Vyzier pressed something that released some kind of magnet-traveler that captured the enemy in a bubble and sent them into space.

In the moment of quiet that followed, Vyzier said, "This dark planet is called Semitz. This is the planet of reptiles. The dragons have taken over, but lizards dominate here. A long time ago, Semitz was a beautiful planet, but its inhabitants, like humans, destroyed each other, and now all that's left is reptiles."

J. J.'s hair was standing on end. "Oh shit! Holy moly! We almost got killed!"

"We'll be out of here soon. You and I, J. J.... we make a good team. Did...this...scare you a little?"

J. J. tried hard to take a deep breath. "Oh, just a little! I think I lost my *liver* back there—and my eyeballs, my heart, my kidneys, and my fear of heights. Other than that...I'm just fine!" she said, with a major twitch in her left eye.

J. J.'s eyes were so big, they were practically popping out of her head. Her hair was standing straight out in all different directions. They were finally away from the dark planet, traveling through the beautiful and colorful lights of the universe. Once again, Vyzier put on the music of Elvis Presley. Rocking and rolling through the universe, Vyzier's feelings for J. J. were becoming more intense. He was falling hard for J. J., but he was trying hard not to let it show. Finally, they were back on Crystal Planet.

"Let me take you for some relaxation," suggested Vyzier.

He took J. J. to a beautiful crystal dome. Inside the dome was a huge swimming pool. There were also large, tall, upright clear tubes full of different colored water. Angels were swimming up and down in the nude just like mermaids. Some were engaged in sex.

J. J. and Vyzier sat on the large, half-egg-like chairs in the pool, relaxing and talking. J. J. said, "I need to go back to Earth...Zonz. I'm feeling much better now, Vyzier."

Vyzier looked into J. J.'s shining eyes. "Are you sure you're feeling better?"

"Yes, I'm ready to go back and deal with my life again. That is...if I still have a life? God help me! I'm going to say a prayer now."

"What's a prayer?"

"Well...when talking to God, it's Earth's greatest direct wireless connection...I'd like to get back to Earth!"

"Why are you so attached to Earth? What holds your interest there?"

"Are you nuts? Well...I have family...and it's the only life I've ever known, you know...stuff..." She paused, thinking. "Well, I don't really know right now, but I want to go back. I'd like to just wake up on Zonz...on Earth!"

Vyzier said, "Your project has already began, and now you're physically and mentally here and no longer just mentally; that's why you don't wake up there anymore. It's only safe to travel by crystal energy, which we call *cia*, from now on."

"Oh shit! What the heck is this project about? I need to know so I can say yes or no to it. Maybe I wouldn't like it? Maybe it'll be too much for me...I mean I would like to know!"

"Oh, you'll like it all right. You have been doing it for some time now."

"Doing what?"

"Making a big difference. I mean, it's a project that you will...you *must* make a big difference, and you will; I'm sure of it. It will be on a larger magnitude."

"Doing what? Like making real good pizza or something like that? It's real hard on Earth to get real good pizza, especially in California, you know. What kind of difference?"

"I'm not at liberty to discuss that...It's up to Zavor. And, J. J., you *must* cooperate with him; it will be to your advantage."

"It will be to my advantage not to get my brain fried again!" She took a deep breath. "Whatever brain I have left. Yes...yes, I know...I know. So I pretty much have no say in this matter, do I?"

"You have much to learn yet!" said Vyzier.

"If I learn one more thing, everything else in my brain is going to fall out...My memory capacity will go on overload, and I will lose all the things I already know, and then Zavor will have to get someone else for this...ha, ha!"

"Hardy, har, ha...everybody wants to be a comedian. You will be exposed to things that you've never seen before, so be prepared."

"Vyzier, can you stay with me? I want you to stay with me through this entire craziness, OK?"

Vyzier sang, "Just call my name, and I'll be right by your side...ha, ha! Of course I'll be with you! Don't worry!"

"Ha, ha...don't worry! Easy for you to say!"

Vyzier said, "I have so many stories I could tell you to help you understand...you know, J. J."

J. J. stared, her eyes glazed. It was déjà vu.

"No, please, no more stories...I've decided to do this project...whatever it is. I want to do it...I'm ready now."

"Holy moly!" exclaimed Vyzier. "Whaa...what? What did you say? Say what? Sweet apple pie with a monster on the side...what did you say?"

"*Yes*, I'm doing this project. I just decided. Surprised?"

"Shocked! Ha-le-lu-ja! La cucaracha! Wow-wow-wow...we are going to see the Wizard of Oz! Kansas City, here we come!" He began singing and clapping. "La-la Pagliacci..." He couldn't contain his excitement.

"Ha, ha! Please, put a lid on it. I always said I wanted to make a difference, but I never really took any action...I want to take action and make real changes in things that mean a lot to me, and now is a good time. I feel that all the pressure on me has evaporated. No matter what the project is, I will do it! I had an epiphany. What if I had died going through the dark planet? Well, I could have died in the desert too! And also I remember how lonely I was on Earth. I was in desperate need of love; I don't want to rush back to that. I always wanted to open up a restaurant where people could meet, so no one would have to feel the pain of loneliness as I did. I was going to call it 'Talk to Me.' That way, it would be easy for everyone to talk to each other. So many people on Earth are so lonely like I was. So, yes, I want to do this special project!"

A brilliant light appeared, and with it came Zavor.

CHAPTER ELEVEN

Zavor said, "Congratulations, J. J.! Welcome! Come, let's talk." The light was so bright that all she could see was Zavor, who was sitting on cushions that looked like clouds. "So tell me, J. J., how are things on Earth according to you? And please feel free to tell me your every concern and what you would like to see change on Earth."

J. J. said, "Well...things on Earth are done...by the golden rule."

Zavor said, "What do you mean by the 'golden rule'?

"Whoever has the most gold makes the rules." She smiled. "Greed runs Planet Earth. For instance, there's plenty of everything on Earth for every human being to live a happy life, but because of greed, we have a few people who have the most and don't want to share, and the rest who have the least. It's a very big struggle, and that also causes wars on Earth...It's all about greed. There's very little humanity left. It's amazing what people will do for gadgets, money, power, or an experience. Since the Industrial Revolution, history has taught us that humanity becomes more materialistic with each passing decade. People are becoming less important than things, and when that happens, families fall apart and human depravity reaches a new low.

"Things that are being produced, most of them are destroying the human species and the Earth...It's the *greed*.

"Then there's global warming. Life on Earth depends on tiny amounts of the gas ozone, a form of oxygen, which is scattered throughout the middle atmosphere eight to seventeen miles above our planet. This ozone layer is our natural sun block. Without it, we have nothing to shield us from the dangerous ultraviolet rays produced by the sun. In 1985, satellites confirmed the existence a large hole in the ozone layer over Antarctica. And the hole is growing bigger all the time. It's caused by humans on Earth. If you are a small group of people trying to change things, it's too hard. And then you have a percentage of humans that don't even care. They just want to survive. So survival on Planet Earth is a struggle at this time. I'm summarizing, obviously. This is all in a nutshell. Of course, I'd like to change things; many people on Earth would like to change things too. But none of us really have any power—unless you're Oprah, ha, ha! In the scientific journals, scientists have predicted that ten or twenty years from now, there will be many more deaths from different kinds of cancers. Twenty years ago, they predicted all the deaths from cancer that have already occurred from carcinogenic products. People do fundraisers and collect so much money for cancer research, and it has helped somewhat. It's like there is twenty square feet of cement foundation on the ground with very large cracks, and with all the money we all raise and all the new cancers continuing to come, it's like putting a little plastic bandage on these large cracks. There're so many new kinds of cancers developing every moment. And the products that are being produced that are causing these cancers will not stop being produced even if it kills all humans on Planet Earth.

"Products are still and will continue to be produced that are constantly emitting fumes that cause a hole in the ozone and that contribute to global warming. And that's just a little part of the picture.

"The ozone 'hole' is really a reduction in concentration of the ozone high above the Earth in the stratosphere. It is a thinning of the ozone layer over Antarctica, caused by stratospheric chlorine, generally called CFCs, or chlorofluorocarbon compounds, which are by-products of some chemical processes. These were also used in air-conditioning/cooling units, and they were also used as aerosol propellants. What makes

CFCs so effective in breaking down ozone is that one CFC radical acts as a catalyst and can break down many ozone molecules. Furthermore, these radicals stay in the atmosphere for a very long time and continue to destroy the ozone with UV radiation being involved in both the natural production and destruction of the ozone layer. The stratospheric ozone layer shields the planet from the UV radiation of the sun. UV radiation causes different levels of cancers and presents a significant health risk, especially for children with asthma. It also damages crops, trees, and other vegetation."

Zavor said, "Hmm...we want you to change things on Zonz!"

J. J.'s eyes were popping out of her head. "Give me a very large magic wand!"

Zavor laughed. "Ha, ha! Yes, we will help you do this project, J. J.! And yes, you'll get a magic wand when you are ready! First, we'll show you how things are done here on Crystal Planet, that is, the things that you need to see. Your earthly pattern is different than ours, so we have to translate our pattern to yours in order for you to see what we have here so you will understand. I now know that you really want to do this project. I can see this in your soul so...where there's a will, there's a way. Don't you worry!" He smiled. "Trust me! Ha, ha. I'm sure you have many questions, and I will always answer them for you. Ask me anything you want."

"What? In five minutes or less? Ha, ha. Yes, I do have so many questions. Let me think. Oh yes...ah...why is this little dog following me?"

"He's your bodyguard! His name is Teeki."

J. J. looked at the dog. "Say what? Ah...my questions really have nothing to do with this dog."

"I know. Don't worry. We have time. Chin-Chin will show you things you need to see. She'll take you around." He pointed at a young lady.

"I have a question," said J. J. "Is this planet in the Milky Way galaxy? What kind of planet is this, and where in the universe is Crystal Planet?"

Zavor said, "This planet is a planimo; it is independent of other planets. For example, Earth and its surrounding planets gravitate to the star you call the sun, and they all gravitate eventually to the center of the Milky Way galaxy. Crystal Planet does not gravitate anywhere. We have built a gigantic shell around our star as a way to harness the star's energy efficiently. Therefore, our planet flows through the universe by itself.

"We've learned how to use the crystal energy to run the planet, and it's conducive to heat or cold as needed as we float through space. It has sort of a spin-stabilizing effect that either increases or decreases heat. It automatically controls our temperature as we need it. We do not travel. We float through the universe independently."

✳ ✳ ✳

Chin-Chin seemed to be a teenager or a young lady. She came close and smiled at J. J. And now, J. J. was left with Chin-Chin and this little dog named Teeki. Zavor had disappeared. Vyzier joined J. J., Chin-Chin, and Teeki.

Vyzier said, "Hi, J. J.! How are you feeling? Confused? Scared? Shocked? Ha, ha!"

"All of the above and more, and I don't know why, but I'm ready for it all. Can you believe this? Please tell me if I've finally lost my mind! I guess Earth has one single pattern, which is human beings, animals, grass, and trees. That is all my brain can translate, and so that's all I'm able to see. Crystal Planet has how many patterns?"

"We have many patterns here, and we're all able to translate them all...including the pattern from Earth. Our brains are more developed than the human brain. You will see things a little bit at a time. Otherwise, it will overwhelm you. Trust me. And no, you have not lost your mind. I would have found it by now. Ha, ha." He laughed.

Chin-Chin was making squeaky sounds and gesturing for J. J. to follow her into a beautiful, clear crystal bubble. It looked a bit like a very large, round spinning top. The dog followed too. They all got in. Just as the spinning top or bubble started to flow into the air, Vyzier stopped them and gave J. J. a pair of glasses to wear.

Vyzier said, "J. J., you're in good hands with Chin-Chin. She'll show you around. You should wear these glasses until your eyes and your brain get used to it, so the things you see will make sense to you. These glasses will translate the pattern for you. After a while, you won't need the glasses anymore; your brain will adjust. I'll find you later, and we'll go over whatever questions you have. Ciao, bella!" He waved at J. J. and disappeared.

* * *

As they flowed through the air, Chin-Chin showed J. J. all these beautiful sights like huge crystal bubbles or domes, which were all lit up with different colors. They were large—about the size of a house—and they were all around. Everything was made of crystal, and J. J. could see reflections of all the different colors.

There were so many sparkling stars and angels flying all around. J. J. looked on in amazement. They stopped in an open crystal gate, stepped out of the bubble, and walked into something like a park. J. J. was wearing her glasses. Everything around was made of different-colors of crystal. The trees had huge leaves, the size of umbrellas. Vines wrapped around and into the crystals; the roots were in huge, long, see-through bubbles full of liquid, and one could actually see all the roots, which were a little off-white in color. Something was swimming around the roots.

It was like that movie when Superman went to his home planet but much more colorful and beautiful. There were plants with huge leaves, one higher than the other (like steps) all around. The huge flowers were as big as a person. There were lines like long straight sticks in the air, and J. J. tried to touch. It was like the stick J. J. had taken once before in what she thought was a dream, but Chin-Chin stopped her.

"No, don't touch the cracks!" Chin-Chin explained the cracks were different dimensions, and they were not to be touched.

Suddenly, J. J. realized there was very little gravity, and she could float. J. J. floated four feet above the ground. She was scared at first, but after balancing herself with her arms and adjusting to it, she liked it. Chin-Chin slowly spread her wings (like an angel) while smiling very comfortably. She was cute and nice, not at all pretentious. She flew all around J. J.

Now, J. J. looked at Teeki (the dog), thinking that he was going to fly too, but, no, Teeki stood very close to J. J. on the ground.

Suddenly, these shimmering bits of matter appeared, like shining dust or glitter that J. J. could only see with these glasses on. The matter formed into the figures of beautiful angels and unicorns who were all flying around this park-like place, and J. J. couldn't contain her excitement.

While looking straight up, J. J. saw these beautiful, shining stars passing through the sky. Suddenly, all these different lights were flashing in the sky, and Vyzier came back and took them into one of the crystal domes.

"There might be enemies from another planet close by, and we need to prepare, just in case we have to attack," he explained to J. J.

The entire planet was lit up now and remained that way until the assumed enemy passed. J. J. could see outside that everything was lit up. All these huge lights; one couldn't see anything else. They all gathered in the dome, and automatically all the crystal domes lowered to be underground.

J. J., who hadn't quite recovered yet, now looked pale and felt very faint. "All these lights... they must run up a heck of an electric bill? Ha."

Vyzier answered her. "Actually, this planet runs on crystal energy. After the alarm is over, J. J., I'll take you to Earth to totally recover, and when you're better, I'll bring you back. All this is a little too much for you to take in right now. When you get a little stronger, I'll bring you back, and you will take up where you left off. OK?"

"No, Doc, I'd like to see more...I know it would be nice to go home for a little while, but I have so many questions I want to ask Zavor. I'm just getting excited to see all these different things on this planet."

All the matter came together and formed into the figures of gorgeous, young-looking males, their skin all different colors. Some looked like Egyptians, and some Europeans. Some were very dark, some very light, and others had snake-like skin. The rest were all different colors. They were all very serious as they flew into domes, preparing for an attack, making some serious sounds, like orders to fire or something.

Zavor appeared. "J. J., you will return to Zonz—Earth—for now. Anytime you have questions, call my name, and I'll answer you."

"You mean, just say your name...or how do I call you?"

"Yes, that is OK. Listen for my voice, and you will see me...only you can see and hear me on Earth. Remember that."

CHAPTER TWELVE

J. J. and Vyzier arrived on Earth, at the beach. Something in J. J.'s bag was moving. When she opened it, out came Teeki. Suddenly, Chin-Chin appeared, calling Teeki. She picked up Teeki, held him, and hugged him. J. J. was surprised that both Chin-Chin and Teeki were on Earth. J. J. knew that Vyzier was coming, but she didn't know about the others. Now they were figuring out how to go home without anyone noticing, since J. J.'s clone was still there.

J. J. said, "Let's all go home and sneak into my room. We can take it from there."

They all agreed. When they arrived and went into J. J.'s room, Phoebe, who had no knowledge whatsoever of J. J.'s being on Crystal Planet or having a clone, saw them and was surprised since J. J.'s clone had just left the house looking picture perfect. The real J. J. looked pale, much thinner, and like she'd been through a war.

Phoebe exclaimed, "J. J.! What happened to you? Are you OK?" She had a shocked look on her face.

"Please, Phoebe," J. J. pleaded. "Come in and sit down and don't say a word. Just listen, OK? I want you to meet Vyzier, Chin-Chin, and Teeki. They're staying with me, and we have to figure out a way so that no one will know that there's me and my clone. My clone and I cannot be seen together!"

Phoebe's eyes were popping out of her head. "What are you saying? You have a *clone*?"

Vyzier spoke up. "Yes, Phoebe, and please don't tell anyone. We need your help with this temporary situation. And it is just temporary, OK?"

"You mean to say that the J. J. who just left is your clone? She's so trim and prim. Oooh...I should have known! Oh my God!" she exclaimed, scratching and shaking her head. "I need a margarita! Maybe a bottle of margaritas!"

They all sat on the bed and talked. The dog sat on Chin-Chin's lap.

J. J. explained to Phoebe all that had happened to her and how she needed all the help Phoebe could give her.

"We'll tell everyone that Chin-Chin is my cousin and Vyzier is a good friend visiting me. Chin-Chin can sleep in my room...Wait a minute. My room belongs to my clone. I'm going to set up a bed in the closet for myself, and Vyzier can sleep in the back. We have to clean it up first. Can

Chin-Chin sleep in your room, Phoebe? And by the way, Chin-Chin doesn't speak English very well. We'll have to teach her."

"Yes...of course," said Phoebe. "Chin-Chin can sleep in my room! Oh my God! I have to wrap my head around this. Whoa. I need a stiff drink, something really strong."

"Please don't tell anyone of this, OK, Phoebe?" J. J. asked.

"Of course not! Who would believe me?" she said, spreading her arms out and then holding her face in her hands. Her eyes were popping out of her head.

Vyzier said, "Phoebe, it's going to be OK. Trust me! Trust me! It's all good."

✳ ✳ ✳

In the kitchen, Phoebe was serving tea and cookies to Vyzier and Chin-Chin, when J. J. came out of the shower in her bathrobe with a towel wrapped around her head. Phoebe told J. J. all that had happened while she was gone.

Phoebe said, "Yes, your clone goes to work and pays all the bills, and she has a serious boyfriend. His name is Sid, and he's coming over to take her out tonight. He's crazy about her. I think he wants to marry her. By the way, Danielle joined the army. Don't ask me why."

"You know, I will miss Danielle. I hope she's safe. My clone has been here only a short time, and she has a serious boyfriend who wants to marry her? I spend my whole life here on Earth, and I don't have a boyfriend or a lover? How the heck did she do that? That's soooo not fair..."

"You got me, babe!" Vyzier sang, looking at J. J. He laughed. "You got me to hold your hand," he added, a loving expression in his eyes.

"Funny guy, Vyzier! About your singing, keep your day job. Ha, ha! Seriously, I'm so tired that I could sleep for a week!"

Vyzier was being skittish, but both he and J. J. now sensed the expanding sexual awareness between them, which was as untamed as their longing for each other.

Vyzier had intense feelings for J. J. He was always joking, but he had very deep feelings for her.

Phoebe took Chin-Chin shopping for new clothes, and J. J. went to the beach. J. J.'s feelings for Vyzier were strong, and she could not control all the butterflies.

While her heart was yearning and her body was aching for Vyzier, she was feeling lost and sad, thinking that Zavor might send her back to the lizards if he found out how she felt about Vyzier. With all the men on Earth, she had to go to another planet and fall in love with an extraterrestrial.

So she went for a walk on the beach. The sun was just setting into the ocean. In her long white dress and large shawl, J. J. walked with her sadness. It was a bit windy.

Vyzier came after her. At this point, he could no longer hide his lustful feelings for her, although Zavor had forbid him from pursuing her. He saw her walking on the shore and called her name, running toward her.

She saw him coming closer. The wind was blowing away her shawl. She lifted up her arms to hold the shawl above her shoulders.

The wind was blowing it away. By that time, Vyzier was embracing her madly, and they held each other tight. Whose caresses incited passion, and whose fiery kisses tantalized?

Even though J. J. was in peril of losing herself completely to this dizzying swirl of temptation, even greater danger threatened to overtake her love. All their hunger for each other had now come to the point of no return. They fed upon each other, lying on the wet sand, not caring about the waves splashing their now wet and sandy bodies.

It was getting darker and the stars were coming out. There was thunder in the sky. They ran under some bushes nearby, where they continued to express their passion for each other.

Vyzier's lifted up his head. "I think the lightning struck me. I feel all this electricity all over my body, or is it our pheromones mingling?" He smiled.

J. J. reached out to Vyzier's neck and pulled him down.

Vyzier said, "If this is foreplay, I'm a dead dude!" he said as he went down.

A little while later, there was a massive clap of thunder, followed by a tremendous bolt of lightning, which was accompanied by even more thunder rumbling in the distance. Like veins, the lightning streaked through the sky.

J. J. asked, "Is that lightning going to strike us? You think it's dangerous to be here? Or is that Zavor? You think we're going to be visiting the lizards tonight?"

Vyzier said, "Oh, what the heck! I think my brain is on fire!" He moved his shoulders up. "Nothing else matters to me now, except you, J. J. I love you." He held her tight and showered her with his fiery kisses.

✳ ✳ ✳

The morning after, they woke up on the sand behind the bushes, half covered by J. J.'s shawl. Vyzier was looking at her face, holding her in his arms when she started to open her eyes. They smiled at each other. They heard a clapping sound and looked all the way up to see a group of people of different ages from a yoga class on the beach staring at them. One older gentleman was happily clapping for them.

Vyzier pulled the cover over their heads, and they both straightened up and walked away, hand in hand. While they were walking, Vyzier told J. J., "I think last night our pheromones were mingling or the lightning struck my brain and turned it into fried pork sausage. It's fried to a crisp...All I care about is you, J. J. I don't care about anything else today."

They sat down together on a bench. Vyzier told J. J., "Be ready to come back to Crystal Planet soon...right after the Razzus attack."

"Who are the Razzu?"

"They are a robot race." He let J. J. see it on a large screen. "Many centuries past, there was this Soclo...He was a genius and created these robots with the genes of reproductive reptiles and the intelligence of the most high-tech computers. Over the centuries, the robots took over the planet Olura, their planet, and they became very aggressive and destructive. They began to take over other planets. They tried to take over Crystal Planet but lost, and now they're trying again." He showed J. J. the battle with the robots as if she were there.

"The reptiles have regenerative abilities? What do they do for them?"

"You cut off their head, and they grow another one. Same with all their parts. It's hard to kill them because they regenerate whatever part was injured or cut off."

"So how do you get rid of them?"

Vyzier said, "We invented kind of a genie in a bottle. It creates a large cloud that kills their regenerative genes and disables the movements in their robotic system." He handed J. J. a bracelet-like device that affixed itself to her wrist and functioned like a phone.

"J. J., this is your traveling tool and a way to communicate with me and Zavor. It's called Cia!"

"Is this a phone? C-I-A? Like the secret service?"

"*No*! Cia, like the crystal energy I told you about earlier. You will travel via crystal energy. With your Cia, you just say the destination, and it takes you there. First put your fingerprint and your vibes on it so no one else can use this Cia but you."

"Whaaaa?"

"You know I have to get back to Crystal Planet, right?" He put his arms around her shoulders. "I will see you soon...and I will take you back with me to Crystal Planet, right?"

They hugged and kissed, and then he left.

J. J. called Zavor on her new Cia device. "Zavor, I need help with this project...I can't do it alone...I need some direction!"

Zavor said, "You will have two angels to guide and help you at this time. One's name is Nova, and the other is Plato, but he wants to be called John. They will come soon, and they will call you."

✳ ✳ ✳

J. J. was now left alone, and she couldn't wait to try using the Cia, her traveling tool. She took Teeki with her, said a destination, and presto! She was in Central Park in New York City. She so elated, like a child with a new toy.

"Wow...this really works!" She walked in Central Park near the boats for a while. "Oh boy, all the places I could go with this!" She was smiling in excitement.

A man tried to steal J. J.'s device, and Teeki turned into a huge monster dog and growled. The men ran away like mad.

J. J. looked at Teeki and smiled in amazement. "Good dog, Teeki. You're great! I better go home and tell Phoebe that I will be gone for a while."

Presto! J. J. was back at home in the kitchen where Sid was sitting drinking coffee and waiting for J. J.'s clone.

J. J. was wearing blue jeans when she entered the kitchen. She excused herself and went to the bedroom. Almost immediately out came J. J.'s clone in a purple-and-black dress. She was all dressed up with her hair up. Sid did a double-take and wondered how she got so dressed up and styled so fast. He was totally stunned and amazed.

"J. J., how did you do that?"

J. J.'s clone said, "Do what?"

Sid was taken aback with a stunned look on his face, and they left to go to a club.

Phoebe said, "Hi! J. J., you should have seen Sid's face!" She laughed. "You two are going to drive him crazy."

"Oh well, I'm going to have a chat with my clone when I have time. I'm going to be in and out most of the time, so don't be surprised if you can't find me all the time. You can call me on my cell if you need me. I'm leaving you in charge, Phoebe."

Phoebe said, "Not with your clone around. She's so meticulous that sometimes she makes me puke. Nothing around here surprises me anymore. Shocks me, yes, but not surprises." She smiled. "But I know what you mean, and I will look after things. Don't worry so much. Should I ask what's going on with you?"

J. J. said, "When I figure out what I'm doing, I'll let you know. I'm so glad you're my friend. Believe me—I don't know what I'd do without you, Phoebe."

"Chin-Chin only eats leaves. Did you know that?"

"Maybe she's a vegetarian! How is she doing? Has she learned any new words yet?"

"Yes, she's so sweet; she's a real pleasure. She's so curious, so inquisitive, and very nice to have around."

✳ ✳ ✳

While Chin-Chin was learning the ways of Planet Earth, she'd been having many adventures. She was also interacting with people. She had been collecting leaves from the bush in the backyard, and a good-looking young gardener, named Eduardo, had been noticing and watching her. He seemed to like her. He smiled and hid from her to see what she was up to. He was very curious about what she was going to do with all those leaves that she'd been putting in a paper bag. She would take them inside the house and come back for more. Finally, he decided to approach her. He dusted himself off and fixed his hair. He straightened himself out with such control and with a big smile on his face.

"Hi there. My name is Eduardo. You can call me Ed. I'm the gardener."

"You can call me C. C." She giggled softly.

"I saw you taking some leaves. What do you need all those leaves for? What do you do with them?"

Chin-Chin said, "I like them." She shrugged her shoulders.

"I haven't seen you here before. Are you visiting?"

"Yes...I'm visiting."

Once C.C. started talking to him, his control evaporated. His heartbeat accelerated as he continued talking to her, and all the while, his eyes were totally checking her out. As she looked at him, he found her a bit intimidating, somewhat mysterious, and very enticing.

Eduardo gave C.C. a red rose. "For you, C.C."

"Hmm, so pretty!" she murmured.

"You want to sit over there and talk for a little while?"

They sat down on a bench under the willow tree and talked.

"When are you leaving?" Eduardo asked.

"I don't know for sure."

"I'm staying with my aunt for a while. I'm adopted, and my adoptive parents died in a car crash. I don't know how long I'll be staying with my aunt. I'm kind of soul searching right now, you know? Kind of a little lost. Sometimes, my past haunts me, and I get depressed."

"You can only take one day at a time," she responded.

"Easy for you to say."

"Yesterday is a lesson learned. Tomorrow is the future, an adventure. Today is a gift; that's why it's called the 'present.' Just remember that."

He looked into her eyes and felt very comfortable pouring his heart out to her.

CHAPTER THIRTEEN

Coach George phoned Charles. "Hi, Charles. How are things going with you and your dad?"

"Hi, Coach. Every time I get ready to tell my parents that I'm gay, I start to have pains in my stomach."

"Is your life worth living this way?" the coach asked.

"No, sometimes I feel like I'm dying inside."

"Well, then just come out and say it. Tell your parents. Take the bandage off; it will hurt much less than it's hurting you now. Just do it and see what happens. If anything, you'll feel better than you were feeling all this time, right?"

"I'm going to do it, Coach. I promise."

They hung up.

Later, Charles was playing ball with his brother, Billy, in the backyard. Charles looked closely at his brother and decided to tell him the dark secret he had been carrying with him all his life.

"Billy, what would you say if I told you that I'm gay?"

"I know you're gay," said Billy.

"What? How do you know?"

His mother (who had blond hair, fair white skin, and was about five feet, five inches tall) walked over to them and looked at Charles, smiling. "I was wondering when you were going to tell me."

"Does Dad know too?" Charles asked.

His mother hugged him. "You have to talk to him and find out. It's a delicate subject for your father, so I really don't know."

Charles was stunned at the news that his mother and brother knew. "I'm going on the fishing trip with Dad, so I'll talk to him about this then. Oh my God, I feel so relieved that you and Billy know," he said, taking a deep breath.

✳ ✳ ✳

On the lake, Charles and his father were getting ready to start fishing. His father was a very good-looking African-American man, over six feet tall with a bulky build, gray hair, and a deep voice. Charles stood there looking at his father, unable to say a word.

"Charles, are you OK? What's up, kid?"

Charles finally mustered up the courage to tell his father. "I'm gay, Dad," he said very loudly, staring directly into his father's eyes.

His father put the fishing pole down, went back to the truck, and sat in the front seat. Charles followed. He stood in front of his father, saying, "Are you ashamed of me, Dad?" Tears were running down his face.

His father got out of the truck and started to walk around. After taking a few deep breaths, he put one hand on Charles's shoulder and said, "I always knew you were gay, son, and I thought it was my fault because I wasn't around much to play with you and guide you when you were growing up. I've been feeling guilty about this for a long time." Tears were also running down his face, and he hugged his son. "Will you forgive me, Charles?"

"There's nothing wrong with being gay or being straight, so there's nothing to forgive, Dad. You didn't do anything wrong. Just like you were born straight, I was born gay. That's just the way we were born. But all this time I was feeling ashamed because I'm not like you."

They hugged some more, and his father said, "You are not like me; you are better than me. Son, I love you, and I'm proud of you."

They ended their embrace and then went fishing together, laughing and joking around. Charles seemed to have a permanent smile on his face, just like a kid playing with his dad.

✳ ✳ ✳

Coach George was on the phone with Ronny. "Hi, Ronny. How are things going with you and your wife? Last time I spoke with you, you were thinking of divorce."

"Hi, Coach. Well, I was thinking about how you told me to record how I was going to approach her with that decision, so I taped my end of the conversation. When I listened to my own voice and heard myself talk, I realized how stupid I sounded. It made me realize that I really didn't want a divorce. I remembered all the good times we had together, and she still looks good. I don't want her to mock my ideas. I do want her support with my work. I was thinking only of myself and what I wanted. So I decided to talk to her in a nice way about things that I would like for her to change, and she was very nice about it. She's happy that I talked to her about all this. She went out and got a haircut, and I took her shopping and bought her some new clothes. She looks nice, and she's looking for a part-time job now. So life is sweet again. Thanks, Coach. I appreciate your help."

"Well, I'm happy everything worked out for both of you. Talk to you later."

They got off the phone.

✳ ✳ ✳

Coach George was on the phone with Barbara. "Hi, Barbara. How are you and the kids?"

Barbara responded, "Everything is so much better now that my husband finally agreed to a divorce. His trucking company is moving to Arizona, and he's moving with them. I just got a small apartment near my sister, and the kids love it there. He moved out already, and we are in the process of moving. My sister and her husband are helping us."

"Did you ever speak to your mother about your issues?" the coach asked.

"I did, and she always responded with the same answer: to forget about the past. She'll never change. One good thing did come out of my conversations with her. I was visiting her, and she told me she liked my hair and that she made me my favorite dish for lunch. I know for someone else, this would be nothing, but for me, it's a drop of the love that I so desperately needed from her. Maybe it's a start. I took a communications class that is also helping me with building up my self-confidence. It's also how you communicate with yourself that helps you be more positive. I made myself a very positive affirmation tape, and I listen to it before I go to bed and first thing when I wake up in the mornings. I'm so relieved, and after all the tragic beatings, I'm finally feeling happy now. You have no idea how much you helped me, Coach."

The coach smiled. "I'm so glad things are better for you and your kids, and you know that I'm always here for you, Barbara. Call me anytime."

She replied, "Thank you so much, Coach. I will call you. Bye."

The call ended.

※ ※ ※

J. J. said to Phoebe, "We're going to have some visitors staying with us soon. Nova can bunk with me, and John can stay where Vyzier was staying. Vyzier left, but he'll be back every now and then. This place is turning into Grand Central Station!"

Phoebe said, "Tell me about it! Who are they... Nova and John?"

"These two are coming to help save my sanity, I hope...I just hope they don't drive us crazy instead! They're friends of mine."

The phone rang, and it was Nova. She told J. J. that John had landed in New York City, at the Port Authority bus depot. Someone had stolen his cell phone (his Cia), his ID, and everything else he had.

"I'm sorry to hear that. Nova, you can come over and stay here, and I'll go get him. I'll try to find him."

Right after J. J. hung up with Nova, the phone rang again. This time it was John telling J. J. where he was.

"Hi, John! Oh really? You went too far east. You need to come southwest to California. Do you want me to come and get you?"

John said he would find his way over and that he would call her again later for directions if he needed them.

* * *

John was now in a store in San Bernardino County, trying to get some new clothes to replace the dirty clothing he was wearing.

John asked a stranger (a young man like himself, whose name turned out to be Eric) where he could find men's clothes. Eric showed him the men's department and the fitting room.

John tried on some pants and a shirt and wore them out of the store without paying. As John walked out of the store, Eric followed him and all the security guards were looking for them.

The police were also looking. Eric told John to hide and that he would have to pay for the clothes, but John didn't understand what "pay" meant. Eric told him to follow him, and they ran until they reached the end of the parking lot. Eric lifted the sewer plate in the street and said, "Let's get in before the police get us."

When they were at the bottom of the ladder, standing in the sewer pipes, each one was saying, "This way," or "No, this way."

Eric thought, *He's good at direction; he can follow the stars*. Eric followed John through the sewer pipes, and after a while, they finally found an exit.

Out they came. They came out all dirty and covered with grease from the sewer, but they were feeling so proud. They turned around and saw all the people and the police looking the other way and realized they had come out of the same hole they'd gone in.

They quickly ran behind some cars. Eric found his pickup truck, and they both jumped in and drove away. Finally, they were very close to J. J.'s house. John called J. J. on Eric's phone for directions.

"Hi, J. J.! I can't seem to find you, and it's getting dark."

"Where are you? Can you read the sign?"

"No...Wait, I'm on the corner of Peach and Emerald."

"You're close. You just went too far south. You need to turn around and go north."

John was very confused. He said loudly, "I don't know north and south...I'm lost here! Stop with this north and south!"

"Just turn around and make a left on Pier Avenue, and I'll meet you there." Laughing quietly, she hung up the phone. "And he's going to help me save the world? I'm in real trouble now!" She took a deep breath.

On the back patio, J. J. called a meeting with her clone. John finally arrived. Nova and Chin-Chin were already there. They started the meeting.

"We need a plan of action. I need to get used to this new phone Vyzier gave me, and then I will return to Crystal Planet with Chin-Chin. You all need to figure out what you've got to do."

With that, J. J. said the place where she wanted to go, pressed the destination into her Cia, and disappeared.

J. J.'s clone, acting as J. J., was now organizing the group.

John said, "Nova and I need to set up our house in the mountains, just like Crystal Planet, so we can be comfortable, so we can spread our hidden wings and breathe in a very inconspicuous way."

✳ ✳ ✳

Arriving in Central Park in New York City, J. J. was learning how to use her new Cia travel device, which looked like a cell phone. J. J. wondered if it could also take her to Crystal Planet. Appearing and disappearing from place to place on Earth without a plane, J. J. was not just learning how to use the instrument but also having so much fun with it. J. J. called her friend Mary Ann in New York City and asked her if she wanted to go to the special park in Queens where they used to go a long time ago. But J. J. also remembered not to let anyone know about the traveling phone.

J. J. and Mary Ann met in a restaurant and took the subway to Queens. Like they had done when they were young, they both put small pillows under their blouses so they looked pregnant enough to get a seat on the subway.

They got on the crowded subway and somehow got separated by the crowd. They were on the same train but in different cars. J. J. got a seat. After that, all the seats were taken, and there were many people standing up. In the middle of this trip, the train stopped, and the lights were blinking on and off. J. J. realized that the train was going under the East River. She looked out of the window and saw cracks in the tunnel. Water was running down from these cracks. The weather outside was ninety-eight degrees. Inside the train, it was much higher—about a hundred degrees or so. The humidity was so high that J. J. thought she would melt. J. J. wondered how long she'd be stuck there. Standing by the door were a big guy and a little guy next to each other. They were having a problem. The little guy told everyone that the oxygen was getting lower, and the big guy was sucking up too much oxygen with his two very large nostrils. He suggested that the big guy close one nostril. The little guy was standing on his toes and stuck one finger in the big guy's nostril.

Of course, the big guy disagreed, and they put it to a vote.

A lady sitting next to J. J. was praying. J. J. asked her what her religion was, and she said she was becoming religious just now, hoping the train would move. Every one voted, and J. J. also voted to close one nostril because she felt there was very little air and the big guy was sucking up the air like a vacuum cleaner. Finally, the train moved, and they got off. J. J. met with her friend.

"Mary Ann, did you get a seat on the train?"

"NO! Not only didn't I get a seat, but someone stole my pillow!" She was very sarcastic, sweaty, and upset.

J. J. decided that she had had enough of traveling for now. She said good-bye for now to her friend and went home.

CHAPTER FOURTEEN

It was night by the time J. J. returned home. She chatted with John, Nova, and Chin-Chin.

"Before Chin-Chin and I go to Crystal Planet, do you have any advice for me or know what I should watch out for? Tell me what I should know."

"Well, there are so many things you have to learn, but here's one thing. Don't touch the cracks, and if the eyes of the cracks look at you, don't look back."

"What are these cracks? Can you explain them to me, John?"

"You'll have to go over that with Zavor to be safe."

"Don't be afraid of the dark side of Crystal Planet," said Nova. She smiled.

"Well, Zavor, Vyzier, I'm ready anytime you are. Phoebe, take care, OK? Are you ready, Chin-Chin?"

Chin-Chin said, "Yes. Come, Teeki." The dog was next to J. J.

Vyzier appeared and began singing. "Just call my name, and I'll be right by your side...Ha, ha... I'm here to take you away."

Smiling from ear to ear, J. J. embraced Vyzier. After saying their good-byes, Vyzier, J. J., Chin-Chin, and Teeki disappeared.

Arriving on Crystal Planet, Chin-Chin was so happy she spread her wings and flew around, feeling free in her own environment.

The horizon was breathtaking it was so beautiful. J. J. could see other planets close by. One was yellow and orange, and the other one was a huge, dark-purple and lavender planet. A white cloud with bright lights appeared with Zavor.

"Welcome, J. J. You look well and rested. Are you ready for us?"

"Yes, as ready as I will ever be." She smiled. "I have so many questions!"

Vyzier said, "While you are on Crystal Planet, wear your glasses until your brain is trained enough to see our patterns."

J. J. put on the glasses and saw all these angels around her, welcoming her. Some stars were sparkling in the sky. The horizon was purple on one side and yellow on the other. J. J. felt very welcome and happy.

Zavor said, "J. J., you are now officially starting your project. Chin-Chin, Teeki, and Vyzier, take J. J. through the crystal to stabilize her oxygen."

Chin-Chin, Teeki, Vyzier, and J. J. all went through the large crystal.

Zavor said, "J. J., you must learn everything you see here on Crystal Planet. It's very important! Let everyone and everything be your teacher."

Vyzier whispered, "Follow the yellow brick road...ha, ha!"

Zavor disappeared, and J. J., Chin-Chin, and Teeki followed Vyzier into a crystal dome. There were large pillows on the floor, and they all sat down to talk.

"There are different sides to Crystal Planet," Vyzier said. "Each side has a different meaning; the dark side is where things are constantly invented and produced. J.J., you need to learn to navigate your own ship to see all the sides of Crystal Planet. Chin-Chin and Teeki will always be with you, and of course, the guide is always in the ship. The guide is called Prazel. Do not fear, my dear J. J., and don't let your eyes pop out of your head...ha, ha! It's all easy. Just call my name, and I'll be busy! Ha, ha!" He was a funny guy.

J. J. was trying hard to be good and was very alert, very serious. Her eyes were popping out a bit, but Vyzier was pushing her buttons and trying to get J. J. to relax and have fun along with learning all these new things on this new planet.

"That's not funny, Vyzier!" she said. "Should I write these things down?"

"No need to write anything down! Ha, ha! J. J., don't worry so much. You'll be fine. Ha, ha! Just relax...I'll keep an eye on you every now and then. I'll call you." He laughed. "There will be a test afterward." He smiled. "There is the bubble over there." He pointed outside the dome with a smile. "That's your ship. Oh yeah, it flies. Let's go!"

Before they all got in the bubble, they stood on this carpet outside in front of the bubble. There was an opening in the bubble, and the carpet lifted up and took them inside the bubble. The inside had all these instruments, like a rocket ship. There were several buttons in the arms of the chairs. One could see outside of the bubble, but no one could see inside. This skinny-looking kind of robot called Prazel was the guide. Vyzier said, "Prazel, meet J. J. She needs to learn how to operate this ship and the meaning of all the different sides. Travel all around Crystal Planet. J. J., I leave you in good hands."

"Vyzier, you're not leaving, are you? Are there any enemies on this planet? Is there anything that could hurt us? Or attack us? Anything I should know?"

"You are safe to travel. Prazel will keep you safe." He smiled.

"What about food and bathroom?"

"This is not a tour of Europe! It's all in this bubble...whatever you want. Just ask and you shall have it. See ya later, alligator." He left.

"I have a fear of heights, tra-la-la!" J. J. shook her head. "Oh well."

The bubble door closed, and off they went. Chin-Chin talked to Prazel in their own language, and Prazel was navigating the ship. Once in a while he looked at J. J. with his cat's eyes. Prazel was a robot, but his emerald-green cat's eyes looked very real.

Chin-Chin said, "Prazel, let's go over the food supplies."

The bubble was flying low over the planet, and J. J. could see huge different-colored domes full of all different kinds of plants and colorful, beautiful flowers surrounded with creatures like large and colorful hummingbirds. It was like an oasis over all the other crystals. After they passed a few domes full of plants, they came to an area full of angels flying all around as if they were dancing to music. And now they came to the educational domes where all these different human-like people, some with different-shaped heads, of all different ages and all different colors, were learning something. Suddenly, Prazel talked to J. J. in his language, and Chin-Chin told him something, and he started speaking English.

Prazel said, "J. J., come. I'll teach you how to fly this ship."

J. J. smiled, and a little scared, she switched chairs with Prazel and let him teach her. Prazel was showing her and pointing at each instrument, telling J. J. what it did and how it worked.

J. J. said, "Should I write this down? It's going to be hard to remember!"

Prazel said, "No writing anything down...I'll be here to teach you."

J. J. took control, and the bubble started to spin all around. J. J. stopped and handed over the controls back to Prazel. Chin-Chin, Prazel, and Teeki were all laughing while J. J. was really scared. Prazel took hold of the controls, and all was well.

"Is there a bathroom on this ship?" asked J. J. "I have to go!"

Chin-Chin looked at Prazel. "She leaks...ha, ha!"

"Oh my!" Prazel looked J. J. up and down. "Huh!"

"I don't leak...I just have to do number one. Do we have a bathroom here or not? Oh, never mind! I'll go later. It's not a big deal."

Chin-Chin smiled. "It's OK, J. J. Stand over here, and this device will absorb your excess bodily fluids."

After they had traveled all around and seen so many sights, they came to an area where lots of sizzling stars were shining and circling all around so beautifully. They arrived in front of the entrance to the clear crystal dome. They got out of the bubble. Chin-Chin, Teeki, and J. J. went inside the dome. Everything inside was made of clear crystal.

They entered a large courtyard, and there were huge rooms all around, each room for something different. There was a clear path (like an escalator) going up. A young man dressed like Vyzier came out of one of the rooms. His name was Zacorian. J. J. had spoken to him when she first came to Crystal Planet.

"Hi, Zacorian," she said. "We met a little while back. Remember me?"

"Yes, I remember you. I will see you later when I show you the dark space."

J. J. said, "I wanted to ask you why you were shooting at me when I was traveling on the one-person rocket ship back to Earth. Were you trying to kill me?"

Zacorian said, "I shot the enemy that was following you home and trying to kill you. That was the explosion you saw behind you. I must go now, but I will see you soon." He left.

Vyzier said, "Hello? Hello..." He smiled. "Did you get lost?"

"No, we didn't get lost!" J. J. said and smiled, happy to see him. "Where are we?"

Vyzier said, "Home sweet home...ha, ha. We're all going to bathe, rest, eat, and sleep for now."

They all entered the blue light, and there were beds shaped like huge half-eggs, floating in some kind of light-blue fog. They entered this whitish fog where there was a huge swimming pool. Everything was cloaked in fog.

Vyzier, Chin-Chin, and J. J. all got into the pool and had fun. There were different colors and tall, see-through crystal tubes full of water, with beautiful angels swimming up and down, totally nude, just like mermaids. Some were making love, and some were seemingly playing. These tall tubes were all around the swimming pool.

When they came out of the pool, they all put robes on and went to sit on huge, silver-white pillows. Vyzier and Chin-Chin drank large cups of green liquid, and J. J. ate leaf cookies and sipped tea.

Afterward, they each went into a floating half-egg to sleep, including Teeki, who slept next to Chin-Chin in a small half-egg.

The next morning, everything was in a light fog, which was peach colored. J. J. put on a long, white dress that draped her body. J. J. was always wearing her glasses. They stepped out onto this beautiful garden and started to float up into the air as if there were no gravity.

Under a very beautiful, very tall tree that looked like a weeping willow with longer, shinier, iridescent leaves, Chin-Chin put her arms straight up and flew up through the leaves, going up toward the light. J. J. followed and so did Vyzier. It was as if the tree was hugging and playing with them. While they were all meditating, they let the leaves touch their faces and their arms, just enjoying the moment and relaxing while the large hummingbirds buzzed all around them.

After a while, they all came down with the hummingbirds following them. They were all laughing and joking.

Vyzier said, "Let's go, gang—up and away, TWA. We've got places to go, people to see, things to learn..."

"Are we going back in the rocket ship with Pretzel?" asked J. J.

Chin-Chin smiled and said, "Don't call him Pretzel; he wouldn't listen to you then...ha, ha. His name is P-r-a-z-e-l!"

Outside of the dome, Chin-Chin, Teeki, and J. J. all stood on a carpet. Soon, the rocket ship came, and the carpet flew up to the ship's door, which opened up to allow them entrance, and in the ship they went. J. J. was learning how to navigate the ship. She took control, and Prazel watched.

J. J. said, "The blue button is up, and the purple is straight...right?"

They arrived at the copper-colored dome where Chin-Chin had asked J. J. to take them. They stopped the ship and got out. J. J. followed Chin-Chin into the dome, which contained so many different clothes. Chin-Chin picked out some clothes and handed them to J. J. to try on. J. J. wore these beautiful, loose, flowing, almost see-through clothes. Chin-Chin tried on some new clothes too. The shoes were beautiful, and they made J. J. feel like she was walking on air. They were so soft and incredibly comfortable, and they hugged J. J.'s feet. The style was simply beautiful.

"I'm going to call the shoes Zonz shoes, OK, Chin-Chin?"

"Yes...ha, ha, OK."

"How much are these clothes? And how much are the shoes?" asked J. J. "I don't have any money with me."

Chin-Chin said, "We don't use money on Crystal Planet. Everything is free."

"Ha! What? You're kidding me. Tell me you're joking!"

Chin-Chin said, "For real...no joking."

They both got back into the ship, and they went to a new location. They stopped in front of another very beautiful, shining crystal dome. They went in, and it looked like there were so many different people, of all different colors and features and dressed in a variety of styles. There were people of all different ages. Everyone was talking to each other in a very pleasant and cordial way.

✳ ✳ ✳

Back on Earth, up on the Santa Monica hills, in a crystal dome that John and Nova had created, J. J.'s clone was getting to know John and Nova. They were all trying to put together a plan of action. Mostly, they tried to figure out how they could best go about stopping the pollution that was harming the Earth's ozone layer.

John asked J. J.'s clone, "The best way to plan these ideas is to have clear communication with ourselves and with others. By the way, where were you last night? I was looking for you."

"I was at...Talk to Me!"

"I am talking to you? *Where were you last night*?" John repeated with big eyes.

"At Talk to Me!"

John said, "I *am* talking to you! I'm communicating with you! *Where were you last night*?"

Nova thought, *This is like an Abbot and Costello sketch*. Nova was laughing, and John was getting irritated and upset.

"I am communicating with you!" the clone said.

Holding his head, John said, "I just want to know where you went last night."

"I went to a restaurant called Talk to Me! You get it?"

CHAPTER FIFTEEN

The TV news was reporting that a bomb had exploded and destroyed a large part of New York City. It was part of a terrorist attack, and many people had died. There were many others crying for their loved ones who were now dead. Another report stated that many Americans had died in the Middle East wars. They were also showing images of all those families crying for their dead soldiers.

"Oh my God. Many presidents have tried and failed," said J. J.'s clone. "How do we fix this? Bringing peace to Earth is really tough."

John said, "Not to mention fixing the ozone. The leaders on this Earth should stop all the destruction...They should comprehend the after-effect of these actions."

"I hope J. J. gets back with a plan of action that will work," said the clone.

✳ ✳ ✳

Back on Crystal Planet, J. J. was asking Chin-Chin all kinds of questions about all these different people and what they were doing.

Chin-Chin said, "They are all instructors and teachers. They've been learning, and now they are ready to teach others. Each one has a special passion, and because it's a passion, it is not work. While they teach others, they're producing something to benefit all of us."

J. J. asked, "Does everyone who works or has a passion produce something?"

"Yes, we all do something. Come, let's go to the ship. There's so much more for you to see."

As the round ship (the bubble) flew over all these domes, J. J. learned that each dome was for a specific purpose. In the open space, there were other ships (bubbles) flying around. And she could see angels also flying all around. They soon arrived at a dome in which were all these people of all different colors, shapes, and features and all different species. They were all participating in processing leaves. It looked like they were making some kind of food. They were all authentically, sufficiently succeeding in producing a food supply for the living creatures on Crystal Planet.

All those who lived on Crystal Planet apparently had to learn every single thing, and whatever this one thing was, whether their passion or not, they each took turns doing that. But they also knew how to do all the other things as well, and everyone enjoyed what they were doing. There were also times when they had fun. It rotated. In the early morning, the middle of the day, and the evening—they all had fun at different times. They all abided by their own laws of nature and logic. They all seemed bound to a common fate. It seemed that the planet was safe from negativities and negative life.

They arrived in this huge, beautiful park. From a distance, J. J. could see it was surrounded by crystal domes. She could see a stream of water running across the park, shining in the light. There were small crystal rocks on each side of the stream that were all made of different colored crystals or maybe diamonds, and beautiful angels were flying as if they were playing in a spectacular panorama. Some bubbles were there, and some angels were floating on clouds.

J. J. wondered if this was heaven. There were vines full of flowers all over the park. It was a very soothing and relaxing place. She could hear very soft music playing; it sounded like angels singing. *Is this where we get our fairytale ideas from?* she wondered.

They got out of the ship, and Chin-Chin spread her wings and went flying like the rest of the angels. J. J. floated on the air, trying to fly like Chin-Chin, but she had no wings. She had seen some straight lines with an eye on top (the cracks).

The eye was like a cat's eye. It was in a triangle on top of a stick with an eye in the middle. Those were the cracks that she had been told not to touch. Her curiosity was running wild, and she had this sudden urge to touch the cracks. As she grabbed one of the cracks, suddenly this strong suction totally vacuumed her into a different dimension, propelling her into a bioluminescent and extraordinarily scary environment. This dreadful multilevel dimension—filled with all different color webs and mosses—was a miasma of some dark and some light colors. Surrounding her were huge webs emitting fumes, odorous gases, and dust. There were loud growling sounds in the background, and winds blew her in different directions, while the atmosphere was constantly changing and so was the temperature. It went from hot to extremely hot to extremely cold. Some unidentifiable but terrifying strange creatures were moving around. It was very frightening being sucked in different directions. J. J. was losing her breath. She started yelling for help while she was being blown up and down by the violent winds. She felt she was being deprived of air.

She heard a loud bark. She saw a huge, overgrown dog, the size of a large monster, coming over. It grabbed her by the arm and dragged her with him. In the middle of all this terror, she nevertheless realized that the huge monster dog was not hurting her, that he was trying to help her, so she hung onto him for dear life. As he carried her, flying through all these different dimensions, the winds were practically blowing her away, and he almost dropped her. She quickly grabbed his ears and held on tight. J. J. felt almost like fainting, but still, she held on tightly, flying like a flag. The strange, strong odor was making her sick, and she was losing her breath. A bright light appeared, and they made it through an opening. They exited that hostile and crazy dimension.

They fell on the ground, safely out of that dimension, away from all the demons and what seemed to be hell. What had appeared like a monster dog turned out to be Teeki, who had come to rescue her. He had saved her life. Teeki turned into his sweet self and sat next to her while they both caught their breath and were able to regain their composure.

J. J. said, "Good dog, Teeki! Good dog! Remind me to get you one heck of a treat! You saved me. You're such a good dog. I love you, baby." She hugged Teeki.

J. J. was dirty. Her clothes were all shredded and stained, some of her hair was cut shorter than the rest, and it was going in all different directions. She had cuts and scrapes all over her arms, legs, and face, and there was a major twitch in her left eye. With her head touching her right shoulder, J. J. got up and tried to balance herself.

"I'm so glad you're with me, Teeki." Dragging her right leg while she walked along with Teeki, J. J. motioned with her left arm up and down, taking a deep breath. "That was no Disneyland!"

They found themselves lost on Crystal Planet. They had lost sight of the park that they had been in prior to J. J. touching the cracks.

Ashamed to call Vyzier or Zavor, she tried to find her way back with Teeki by her side. They sat under a tree, intending to rest and try to figure out what would be the best road to take, but then all the leaves fell on them. They were small tree angels who looked like white and silver leaves.

The sweet little tree angels dragged her to a nearby pond next to the silver falls and dunked her in. They washed her body and her hair so sweetly. The pond was full of a water-like liquid, but as she stepped out of the pond, she realized she wasn't wet at all. The liquid did not wet her. Her body was dry and clean. The little angels replaced her shredded, dirty clothes by covering her up with flowers. They dressed her with large flower petals, all white and silver, petals on top of petals. It made a beautiful dress on her. They flew all around J. J., combed her hair, and patted her face. She felt so much better, but her leg was still dragging.

J. J. felt like a giant princess with all these beautiful little angels taking care of her. She told the little angels that she was lost, and they immediately called out to something. A beautiful, giant, translucent, amber-colored dragonfly came, and all the little angels helped J. J. and Teeki get on top of the dragonfly. She was afraid she might fall off, and she wondered if someone was testing her fear factor. She felt like she was sitting on top of one of the very earliest four-winged airplanes, right after they were first invented. She had no choice, but she kept on falling off and falling on her leg was starting to hurt. The little angels were sort of laughing. This was amusing to everyone but J. J. Some angels came and talked to her, but she didn't understand them. They touched her and smiled. They were very friendly and curious.

A bubble appeared (like the bubble she had traveled in with Chin-Chin). The door opened, and the little angels helped her and Teeki into the bubble. Inside was a beautiful, goddess-like angel sitting in the navigator chair. She introduced herself by saying, "I am Zezra. Don't worry, J. J. I will take you to Chin-Chin."

"You know my name?"

"Yes," Zezra replied. "We all know that you will change Zonz. We're all with you in spirit, J. J."

CHAPTER SIXTEEN

The bubble took J. J. and Teeki to where Chin-Chin was. J. J. thanked Zezra and waved good-bye. Chin-Chin was flying, and when she saw them arrive, she was very happy. Then they all floated around for a while in the park. It was fun. After a while, Chin-Chin and J. J. hugged. J. J. was happy to see her, more than Chin-Chin understood.

Now Chin-Chin and Zacorian joined them in the bubble, and they took off for a higher dome. They entered a city, or so it seemed. They stopped at one particular dome. Inside, it was full of circles. In each circle, there were beautiful female and male angels, very busy and very graceful. The females looked like goddesses, their skin all different colors, and with different features. They were surrounded by scientific instruments, clear tubes, and panels filled with crystal buttons in all different colors. They were all scientists at work. As they walked into the higher level, there were all the people J. J. remembered seeing as a child on the clouds. They all welcomed her. They offered her a large pillow (like a cloud) in the center of them all, and she sat while each one talked to her.

A man called Tammuz, who had a very deep voice, asked, "J. J., do you have any questions?"

"Well, yes...the crystal box you have, the one that heals people when they walk through, is that magic or what kind of technology are you using?"

Annaki answered, "It's not magic. We use crystal energy technology. As you enter the crystal box, as you say, inside it's all one big X-ray machine that sends a picture of the body to our entire scientific division. With our technology, we're able to see every single cell, bone, and vein, everything the body has, individually or altogether. We can see your body and know exactly what needs to be healed or adjusted, and we all work through the crystal box to fix everything. It's just like how your eyes see things upside down and send the message to your brain, and your brain translates and puts it right-side up. It's done so fast you don't realize the process; you just see things like magic. The crystal box works the same. So it's not magic."

"That's brilliant technology! I'd like to learn more."

Tammuz said, "When souls arrive here, we make a clone. It's like on Earth, in the United

States, where everyone needs a Social Security number; here, we make a clone. That way, if some disease starts that we cannot control, we can have the total memory transplanted to the clone, and we learn how to destroy the disease. Our scientists detect all kinds of illnesses and destroy the disease before it spreads. Our scientists have learned that in some cases, they have to do gene-splicing for some animals so they can fly, and that works for us. On Crystal Planet, our brains are fully developed, whereas on Earth, the highest brain development is between one-quarter and two-quarters developed."

"That's true," said J. J. "How can we on Earth develop our brains faster?"

Tammuz said, "Because humans on Earth focus so much on wars and greed, they limit themselves in brain development. In fact, it's not so much brain development as brain destruction, and that mentality destroys the planet as well. Here on Crystal Planet, we all live to help each other, and we develop healthy and strong brains, which help us live up to our potential for a happier life. We all take turns doing what needs to be done. We all have whatever we want. It's all free. When we need something different, we go back again and exchange what we have for what we want or need. We all produce, and we all enjoy. We all go through the crystal box (as you call it) to make sure we're all healthy and to prevent any kind of disease. We all take care of each other,

and we never have what you on Earth call "pov-
erty." We take care of ourselves, each other, and
our beautiful planet.

"That is a rule never to be abused. There is
enough of everything on each planet for everyone to live happily, forever. If all humans focused
on helping each other in making life better for all
humans on Earth, then instead of wasting your
brains and energy, your brains would develop
faster and your environment on Earth would be
ideal. Planet Earth provides you all with so much
abundance and beauty and so much to live for.
Why would you want to destroy that? We have
sent many angels to Earth to help change humans'
mentality, but the earthlings have developed
such a strong and obsessive need for greed. From
this standpoint, all humans must abandon greed,
cynicism, and selfishness. You must all form a
human connectedness as an ultimate energy. This
ultimate universal energy is available to all—it is
a place where everything exists in unity as one
being, one suchness. Stop running from death,
and run to life. That effort is necessary to undif-
ferentiated universal energy. You need to identify
with this aspect, something concrete that can be
contained in your minds. You all contemplate
and activate them in yourself in order to...not just
survive but live in abundance. Then humans and
Planet Earth can both prosper."

Astarte said, "Now, time is of the essence...
to save Planet Earth. Humans have destroyed so

much, including the environment in which you all live. You have some job now, J. J.! We will help you. We will be with you in spirit. Be generous, not greedy; there's no way anyone can express the importance, the urgency, and the magnitude of this change on Earth."

Bast added, "Some scientists on Earth are concerned that a message from outer space could start a panic or create a sense of despair when people realize they are not the most advanced creatures in the universe. Others are just plain scared. That's why we need you to make all these necessary changes on Earth, with us helping and assisting you to save the human race and Planet Earth."

Gaia said, "Prosperity comes when greed and wars stop."

Eurydice said, "Human connectedness is needed on Earth, and it must be achieved to change things on Earth."

Hebe said, "Use your *hearts* to love one another and help each other. In a place of love, hate cannot exist."

Tlazolteotl added, "Ridding yourselves of greed is the first step. No greed will enrich you or enrich the Earth."

"Education and sharing your knowledge is so powerful," said Ishtar.

Ix Chel said, "To continue your existence on Earth, humans must show a systematic trans- formation of a powerful and all-encompassing nature. All humans are responsible for one small aspect of existence in unity."

Valkyrie said, "This civilization must be of peace and beauty."

Sphinx said, "Each human must be a supreme creator of the ultimate universal energy where everything exists in unity as one being."

Unelanuhi addressed J. J. "J. J., you need to take action in all we say."

Persephone warned, "Don't let greed destroy Earth and human life."

They looked at each other and talked to each other in their language. Amphitrite, one of the scientists, turned to J. J. "J. J., you will find a way to accomplish this project. We'll be watching and helping you."

J. J. was somewhat overwhelmed but still very focused, alert, and accepting of this advice. She, C.C., and Zacorian left in the bubble. J. J. navigated the ship. Zacorian told her where to go and showed her the sights.

J. J. asked, "Can I call you Zac?"

"Yes." Zac pointed to a huge courtyard with domes all around and told J. J. a little about it. "We can all have anything we want. After all, we only have one body. If we want something else, we can come back and exchange what we've taken today for something different."

"So you don't need closets and places to store things?"

"No need for that," he answered. "We all have whatever we like and then bring it back and get something else. When we return things, they get cleaned and sterilized so we or someone else can use them again.

"Do any of you pay any kind of taxes or IRS?"

"I don't know what that means, taxes or IRS! No. No one pays for anything. There's no paying for anything anywhere on Crystal Planet."

"I am going to pack up my stuff on Earth and move here to Crystal Planet! Ha, ha!"

They all entered a dome full of clothes, shoes, jewelry, and so many other things that J. J. had never seen before. There were angels, both male and female, helping everyone. J. J. found herself feeling like she was in a wonderland, like a child in a candy store. They also had things to cover up the ears (which they all wore) to regulate sound. Their shoes were made of a hard sponge that grew in some of the crystals. Walking in these shoes was like walking on a cloud.

J. J. and C.C. were now dressed in new clothes. The clothes were all made of a material that was made of flowers. The women's fashions were silky and loose and long, falling almost to the ankles. The robes draped beautifully down over the body to fit its shape. Once dressed, they all went back in the bubble with Zac to see other sights.

Zac took over the navigation, and they went to the home of "the birds." These were bird-people who took care of the trees. They were just like bird families—male birds, female birds, and small children or baby birds. It was amazing.

Zac said, "Let me show you some of our helping animals."

As they traveled through the crystal mountains, it seemed to J. J. that it grew a bit darker. The light had a purple hue. They continued into a valley-like place and arrived in front of an archway of crystal. They got out of the bubble and went in. There was a flying creature that was something between a horse and a lion with wings. Huge birds patrolled the area. There were lots of beautiful flying unicorns, and lots and lots of flowers and different colored crystals all over. There were huge dragonflies, big enough to carry three to four people.

On the horizon, they could see a huge planet. It was partly lavender colored and partly bright purple. It was just like the Garden of Eden. Under the weeping willow, they got to touch the beautiful flying animals. J. J. was kind of afraid of them, but Chin-Chin ran and hugged a huge winged lion and called him by name. It sounded like *Kauki*. Chin-Chin hopped on Kauki, and they went off flying. They circled the area all around J. J. Chin-Chin was so happy. Zac was also happy and was patting some kind of huge beetle that opened up its wings and formed a rectangular multicolored carpet. Zac rode the huge beetle. Chin-Chin came over. She wanted J. J. to go on Kauki with her. She pushed her onto it, and J. J. was so afraid but held on tight to the lion. Off they went. J. J. was screaming, afraid of falling. Chin-Chin found this amusing. There were so many angels, young and old, riding all different kinds of animals. They were flying and playing, having fun with all these beautiful flying animals.

Finally, they got back into the bubble and went onto what looked like a city made of crystal. There were so many angels of all different ages in all groups. These were the schools. They just passed by and went toward the purple light. These domes were where they did cloning. Everyone was assigned to a different group for learning different things. It was amazing and well organized. They were very into what they were doing. Some angels were guarding young children. Some of the children had wings, and some didn't. It was so peaceful and a beautiful thing to see. Overall, they were all enjoying and were happy doing whatever they were doing. They looked like they all had a purpose and they all belonged. They were so happy enjoying doing something together, and no one was left out.

Zac said, "You navigate now, J. J. Did you enjoy the tour? Do you have any questions?"

J. J. said, "Everything looks so beautiful. Is it like this all the time?"

Zac said, "Yes, it's always beautiful—whatever we're doing—and we always have fun. This is what life is about, fun and helping each other. We're never alone, no matter what we do. So we always belong to each other and to our planet, and our planet belongs to us."

Chin-Chin said, "Did you have fun, J. J.? Did you like riding on Kauki?"

J. J. said, "Ha, ha...that was fun. Kauki was so soft. Where's Vyzier? Will he be joining us soon?"

"Yes, soon," Zac said.

Vyzier said, "Here I am!"

✳ ✳ ✳

Vyzier took J. J. into the bubble by herself and showed her his favorite sight.

The stars in the purple sky started to shine, and with the bubble, they went up the crystal hills to where they could almost touch the shining and sparkling stars. Where the purple sky ended, another orange planet began. The dramatic colors around the stars circling the skies were like magic. J. J. felt like she was part of the universe. Vyzier and J.J. got out of the bubble, and they sat facing each other on top of the huge crystal, watching the stars in the sky and just resting there lovingly. Vyzier looked at J. J. in a romantic way.

Vyzier said, "This is what you call romantic, right?"

"Yes, it's very romantic," J. J. said and smiled.

Vyzier asked, "How do you feel about me, J. J.?"

J. J. said, "Well...once, a long time ago, I read this book to a child. It was about a bunny and a duck. There was a little bunny who was with a bunch of bunnies, and yet this bunny had no one to play with. Then the bunny found a large egg and started to play with it. It was a lot of fun rolling the egg down the hill, rolling it into the flowers and over small rocks. One day, the egg started to move. It broke apart, and out came a duck. The bunny said, 'What did you do to my egg? Now you're a duck!'

"So the duck and the bunny played together all the time and had so much fun. They laughed. They chased each other. They played hide-and-seek. One windy day, they got separated and lost. They each found themselves alone in search of the other. Even though the bunny found other bunnies and the duck found other ducks, they were very sad and lonely. Finally, they found each other again, and they were so happy. From then on, they celebrated their life together every day because they knew that in a world full of bunnies and in a world full of ducks, they were not happy. But together, they found happiness. I feel the way the bunny and the duck felt about each other. That's how I feel about you. With you, I'm happy, and without you, I'm sad and miserable."

Vyzier said, "The bunny and the duck—who was the boy and who was the girl?"

J. J. said, "Who cares? It's love!"

Vyzier said, "That's true. I feel the same way about you, J. J. I just wanted to know whether to call you bunny or ducky! Love is the strongest thing in the universe. You got me, babe!"

J. J. sang, "Just call my name...and I'll be by your side...ha, ha."

Vyzier said, "Hey, that's my song, bunny." He smiled.

CHAPTER SEVENTEEN

Later, Vyzier and J. J. joined the others in the bubble and went into the silver dome.

J. J. said, "Zac, are we staying here to sleep?"
Zac said, "Yes, we can go anywhere we like. I think you might like it here. The trees here sort of resemble Earth's a little."

In the center of the dome, there were many wisteria-like trees. They had cascading, soft, silver-green leaves, and the flowers were like upside-down bells made of soft gold. All these huge eggs (each about the length of a human adult's body) lay sideways inside of the flowers. The flowers and eggs resembled a huge chocolate kiss or a teardrop. The large bottom part was the egg's nest. It rested, hanging down from the trees. They opened the egg, and inside was like a soft white cloud. That was a bed in which to sleep in this beautiful garden. The soft golden bells were like chimes, making the most soothing music J. J. had ever heard. It totally relaxed her. The music lulled her so completely that she slept like a baby.

The next morning on Crystal Planet, they all woke up, totally rested and full of energy. They went to the back of the garden, and in the mild, peach-colored fog, there was a very long swimming pool. Many angels were getting in and having fun, and so did they. They came out, and these little white angels began drying them and fixing their hair. They gave them dry clothing. It was like a spa. After they ate leaves and flowers, they went into the bubble. Up they went, traveling through Crystal Planet.

Back on Planet Earth, John was watching the news and saw a report on the war in the Middle East. Many Americans and people from other countries were injured, and so many other people were dead from the never-ending wars. Somebody's father, brother, son, daughter, or husband was dead. Terrorist bombs were going off in many airports. There were subway crashes, and so many people dying. The heat wave was unbearable, and people were dying from that, too. So many fires had sprung up all over the planet. Oil spills were once again destroying life in the sea. Unemployment was at its highest, and people had been and were giving up on the government and on themselves, unable to support and feed their families while a very few people on Earth had it all. John and Nova were totally disgusted by all this.

No one else in the house was interested in watching the news because it was very disturbing and so very depressing. A neighbor had lost her husband in the war, and she herself was dying of cancer. Her four children had no one else.

John said, "I don't understand why no one seems to care. Maybe they just don't know what to do. No one seems to take charge and lead a major change. The government promises to make changes, but things are getting worse."

Nova said, "This requires a major change. We have to get everyone to care or at least, we have to get them to start caring."

✳ ✳ ✳

Back on Crystal Planet, J. J. asked Zac, "What do you do? What is your passion?"

Zac said, "I am a scientist; that's my passion."

Chin-Chin said, "My passion is designing clothes. I'm a fashion designer. I designed what you're wearing, J. J." J. J. was wearing a beautiful, gray, long, loose dress.

"How much does it cost for college here?" asked J. J.

Zac answered, "We all learn everything for free; there is no cost. We all must learn everything, do what our passion is, and develop that to our highest potential. We all have different passions, so we all do different things, but each one of us can do all things. For example, I work in my science lab for a period of time, and then someone else comes and works there, and I do whatever I choose and go wherever I want to go. After one medium, or one week, I go back to the lab, or I go where I'm needed the most. My specialty is science. So there's no money on Crystal Planet. Everyone learns about and works in their passion. Sometimes we will go where we're needed the most."

J. J. said, "I like that. It's taking me some time to comprehend the idea of not paying for anything here. Do you think they, your superiors or Zavor, will assign you to come to Earth with me? Zavor, can Zac come with me to Planet Earth?"

Zavor said, "Yes, J. J. Zac can actually help you, right, Zac?"

"Yes. If you need me on Earth, then I will come with you."

"Vyzier, where are you?" asked J. J.

Vyzier sang, "Just call my name, and I'll be by your side. Ha, ha...I'm always by your side, J. J. Sorry to tell you, J. J., but Danielle joined the army, and they reported her injured while fighting in Iraq. She's either injured or dead.

They're not sure. I'll join you on Earth later."
He hugged J. J. and faded into the fog.

"OK then," J. J. said. She was already missing
Vyzier. "You will be a great help on Earth, Zac. I
want you and Chin-Chin to come to Earth with
me. Maybe we all can find out what happened to
Danielle. If she's still alive, maybe we can save her."

"I am so ready. Let's go!"

✳ ✳ ✳

Back on Earth, J. J., Chin-Chin, Zac, Teeki, and
Vyzier found themselves on the beach.

"Welcome to Planet Earth, Zac!" said J. J.

Zac was looking around and smiling, obviously
ready to get involved. They arrived home and met
John, Nova, J. J.'s clone, and Phoebe. They spent
some time greeting each other, and then sat around
and discussed how to start the plan of action, how to
get to Iraq and find Danielle.

Phoebe said, "Danielle mailed me a post-
card. This is the address where she is staying—or
where she *was*."

J. J. said, "Let's go and find her." She pressed
her Cia, her crystal-energy travel device, and
showed the rest of the gang the address.

J. J., Vyzier, Nova, John, and Zac decided to
go. The rest would stay behind for contact and to
check to find out if anyone knew for sure where
Danielle was.

They all arrived in Iraq, in the middle of the war. Everything around them was being blown to smithereens. So many people were dying, and so many were badly hurt. There were women and children being blown to pieces. John and Nova saved a group of children who had been left all alone and were lost before a bomb exploded. They took them to safety. There were a lot of explosions all around and enough dust to suffocate them. They were all searching through the sick and the dead to see if Danielle was there.

One of the explosions injured J. J., and John tended to her while the others ran to help her to a cave. John tied a board to J. J.'s leg, so she could stand up. They couldn't find Vyzier, who had been in the area where a huge bomb had just exploded. They found Danielle among the dead, and Zac tended to her immediately.

"She's still alive!" Zac yelled. "She's injured very badly, but she's alive. Why are these people attacking? Why are they fighting? What is this war about?"

J. J. said, "We must find Vyzier!" They searched all over. "This war in the Middle East has been going on for so long. Ouch, my leg! I don't know if there will ever be peace in this land. So many people have already died to bring peace, but they're still fighting without end."

Everything was covered with dust from the bombs exploding. The sound of the machine guns was deafening. J. J. finally found Vyzier, who was soaked with blood as if he had been blown up. J. J. was crying, screaming, and yelling at the others to go home. "Please go home now," she begged, "before someone else gets killed!" The others heard J. J. from a distance, but they were unable to see her or Vyzier through the dust. They all listened, grabbed each other, and went home.

J. J. was crying. "Vyzier, are you OK? Are you alive? Stay with me! Don't leave me. This is a mess. Please, Vyzier, stay with me! I will take you to Crystal Planet. Vyzier, please! I'll take care of you." Holding Vyzier, J. J. touched her Cia, her travel device, and they disappeared.

The rest had all gathered, and with the travel device, they took Danielle and the children with them and went home. At home, they called the government agency for the protection of children and turned the children over to the agency. J. J. took Vyzier to Crystal Planet and put him into the crystal box. J. J. was crying loudly and yelling for help.

"Save Vyzier please!" she pleaded. *"Save Vyzier!"*

A very emotional J. J. continued loudly yelling, "Save Vyzier!" Her cries echoed throughout the crystal domes. Inside the crystal box, J. J. was begging, "Please take my heart or any of my parts and give them to Vyzier! Please save Vyzier." J. J. stood up and without stopping, kept yelling, "Save Vyzier!" Zavor was watching all this from his place in a large crystal and saw J. J.'s aura start to enlarge into a huge rainbow of color, as if she were charging up with some kind of energy. All the while, a blue light was coming over to her and shining on Vyzier. It was saving his life, as J. J. had wished.

An emotional J. J. fell to the ground, totally exhausted. Zavor was watching all this in amazement. A lady scientist came and guided two blue men to take J. J. and Vyzier out of the crystal box and to a cloud-like bed, where they both rested.

Later, Vyzier woke up. J. J., looking like a ghost, opened her eyes and saw Vyzier alive. She kissed him all over his face. J. J. and Vyzier were smiling at each other and glad to be alive. Zavor realized the love between the two was very real and very strong, and it couldn't be denied.

Zavor appeared next to J. J. and Vyzier, smiling at both and letting them know that he now approved of their love for each other—a love that was once forbidden.

✳ ✳ ✳

On Planet Earth, they were all discussing the crazy war. Zac was able to help Danielle and mended most of her wounds. Danielle was in bed resting, still unconscious. She needed rest. They all cleaned up and then got together to start a serious discussion about how to change things. Once J. J. and Vyzier came back to Earth, they joined the group. They were holding hands and looking like they'd been through a real war. (Oh yes, they really had.) Phoebe turned on the news. There was a talk-show host talking to someone from Beverly Hills and some of his high-society friends about how many millions they had and their famous clothes designer.

J. J.'s clone said, "This is incredible! We need some kind of balance for the human race. There is no humanity on Planet Earth right now. We will reach the public by going on television and appealing to the rest of the people. Let's talk about what we're going to say. I will go to New York with Zac. I have a friend who works on TV. I think if we televise our goals we can reach a large percentage of people, and that will start changing things. I will find a way to contact a top scientist for Zac to work with in possibly saving the ozone. John and I will go to Los Angeles first and go on this talk show. Let's write what we need to say."

J. J. said, "Phoebe, you will go to the seminar as a guest and ask the coach to announce to the class that we are looking for people who want to join us in this crusade to save the Earth. He should tell them they can contribute to an emerging world. Our goal is to touch as many lives as possible with a message of hope for a better world. Nova and Chin-Chin will go to Washington, DC, and protest to improve the environment. It will be televised. Here are traveling and contacting devices for us all. Do not lose these! Ha, ha. And we each will have a credit card to pay for stuff, necessities only, so that we can eat and stay wherever we need to. First, let's get to the Internet to find groups that we need to contact and associate with. Vyzier and I will go to Washington to see if we can request an appointment to meet with the president of the United States and talk to him about meeting all the different leaders of the world."

J. J. and Vyzier held each other tight and smiled.

Vyzier said, "You and I, Bunny...we'll do it together." He smiled.

J. J. wrapped her arms around his neck. "Yes, Ducky...we will."

✳ ✳ ✳

The group sat inside the crystal dome that Nova and John had built on Earth, and they planned and scheduled. When they were done, they came out of the crystal dome that sat on top of the mountains, all celebrating their togetherness and their ideas about how to change Planet Earth for the better. There were no politics there; this was the real thing. The discussion continued as to how to enlist all the others to help with the project that must take place here and now.

Nova, John, and Chin-Chin all spread their wings and flew around in excitement. The rest were excited to see them fly. After celebrating and getting everything in order, they all left to take action, going in different directions (like heavenly angels).